the

love

pug

the
love
pug

j.j. howard

SCHOLASTIC INC.

Copyright © 2020 by Jennifer Howard
Emojis throughout © i43/Shutterstock.

All rights reserved. Published by Scholastic Inc., *Publishers since 1920*. SCHOLASTIC and associated logos are trademarks and/or registered trademarks of Scholastic Inc.

The publisher does not have any control over and does not assume any responsibility for author or third-party websites or their content.

ISBN 978-1-338-33934-5

10 9 8 7 6 5 4 3 2 1   20 21 22 23 24

Printed in the U.S.A.   40
First printing 2020

Book design by Yaffa Jaskoll

For my mom, who first taught me
to love dogs (. . . *and* cats)

1

The Amazing Cupid

January 1: Cupid has special powers!

As soon as I'd written the words, I frowned. A big blot of ink had leaked from my pen and marred the very first page of my brand-new journal. I could almost hear my friend Theo's voice in my head, teasing me for using an ink pen. But I loved old-fashioned things, even if they took a bit more time. *And sometimes made more of a mess*, I thought as I dabbed at the ink with a tissue.

My adorable pug, Cupid, let out a bark from where he sat on my bedroom floor. I'd been writing at my desk, but I turned around to pull my dog up into my lap. I stroked his soft ears, admiring his tan fur and sweet, wrinkly black muzzle.

"*Do* you have special powers?" I asked Cupid, gazing into his wide dark eyes. He let out a snuffling sound as if to say, *Why, yes, I do, Emma.*

I nodded. It might have been the only explanation for what had happened earlier that day.

My best friend, Hallie, and I had been walking with Cupid down the street to visit my former babysitter, Annie Taylor. Annie is in high school, and she'd offered to help Hallie prepare for the middle school cheer squad auditions.

It was cold and sunny, which is my favorite weather, but Hallie had not been so happy.

"It's freezing," Hallie groaned, nestling herself deeper inside her puffy coat. "Shouldn't we be hibernating on New Year's Day?"

"Okay, gloomy-pants," I told her. "Why can't you be more like Cupid? See how much he's enjoying this awesome weather?"

We both looked down at Cupid, who was walking along between us with a definite spring in his step.

"Yeah, well, I think his coat's warmer than mine," Hallie

said, and I couldn't argue with that. Cupid *was* wearing his warmest outfit—a deep red down jacket trimmed with faux rabbit fur that I'd dressed him in that morning.

"How come you're so grumpy today?" I asked Hallie. Even though I was usually the more cheerful one of the two of us, Hallie didn't usually seem *this* blue.

She sighed. "I guess I'm just not sure about this whole cheer-squad-tryout thing. I mean, I still don't even know if I *want* to be on the team."

"Come on, Hallie, you're going to be great!" I told her confidently. "And with Annie's help, you'll be a lock at the tryouts. She's the team captain at the high school."

"I know, Ems. You've only told me nine thousand times. But that's not what I was saying . . ."

Just then, Cupid began barking excitedly, which was unusual for him. He's more of a laid-back sniffer than a barker, unless he's agitated or very happy.

I looked up to see a moving van parked in front of the house next door to Annie's. She must have been getting new neighbors. I realized that Cupid was barking at the teenage boy who had just pulled a chair out from the back of the truck.

Cupid tugged on his leash, which he also *never* did. I yelped in surprise as the leash slipped out of my gloved hand. Then Cupid shot straight toward the boy.

"Cupid!" I yelled, racing after him.

The boy put down the chair and scooped up Cupid. My pug immediately started giving the boy a series of sloppy licks right on his face. I turned to Hallie in surprise. That was three strange things Cupid had just done, right in a row. Even though he's very affectionate, he doesn't normally "kiss" strangers. He mainly reserves his face licks for me or my neighbor Theo.

Annie, no doubt hearing the commotion, opened her front door and stepped outside. As soon as he saw her, Cupid started to squirm in the boy's arms. The boy let him go, saying to me, "I'm sorry—I was afraid he was going to jump down."

"It's okay," I called, and changed direction, since Cupid was now running straight for Annie. When she saw him on the loose, she started running too, and soon we were all standing in a circle, with Annie holding my very naughty dog, and getting some Cupid face kisses of her own.

Annie giggled. "Emma, your dog is out of control."

"Not usually," I told her, shaking my head, still confused about his odd behavior.

"Hi," the boy said. "I'm Mateo. We're just moving in." He pointed to the house next door to Annie's.

Annie looked up at him (she had to look *up* because he— Mateo—was very tall . . . and very cute) and I swear, the look on her face made it seem like she'd just been struck by lightning.

"I'm Annie," she told Mateo, her voice sounding a little breathless.

The way she was looking at Mateo—and the way he was looking back at her—made me wonder . . . did they *like* each other? I glanced at Hallie, and her smile told me she was wondering the same thing.

I knew Annie didn't have a boyfriend. In a classic move, head cheerleader Annie had dated the quarterback of the high school's football team for two years, but since the breakup with Nate, she had been single.

I looked at my little pug in Annie's arms, and I could almost swear he . . . winked at me. Or maybe he was just blinking. But

Cupid *had* been the one to bring Annie and Mateo together.

Wait a minute. Was he living up to his name?

I stepped forward to take my pug from Annie so she could focus on getting to know Mateo. Though clearly someone needed to actually start the conversation, because they were both just staring at each other.

"Welcome to Highbury, Mateo," I said brightly. "I'm Emma, and this is my best friend, Hallie. Where did you move from?"

Mateo shook his head, like he was remembering where he was, and turned to look at me. "We just moved from Baltimore," he said.

"Wow," Hallie said. "Highbury's going to be a huge change for you, then."

Highbury, Pennsylvania, is a very small town—but that's part of why I love it so much. *Technically* I was born in another town (there's no hospital right in Highbury), but besides that, I've lived here all my life. I've gone to school with almost all the same kids since kindergarten, and I know every part of the town as well as I know my own name. And I love that you don't even really need a car in Highbury—you can walk basically everywhere.

"Highbury is the most wonderful place in the world," I jumped in to tell Mateo.

An idea started forming in my mind. I glanced from Annie back to Mateo. "In fact, to fully appreciate it, you should have a local show you around. Annie, maybe you could help?"

"Oh," Annie said, blushing. "Sure. Are you starting at the high school tomorrow?" she asked Mateo, who nodded.

"I'm a senior," he said. "Still haven't forgiven my parents for moving in the middle of the year."

"Oh no!" Annie said, her eyes going round. "I'm sorry. But Emma's right—Highbury really is a great place, and I'll introduce you to everyone at school. I'm a senior too," she added. "You'll have so many friends before you know it, I promise!"

Cupid gave a short bark of agreement, and we all laughed.

A loud voice came from the driveway next door. "Were you just gonna dip out of the rest of this unloading nightmare or what?" The boy hollering at Mateo was clearly his younger brother. He looked just like him, only shorter.

Mateo frowned at the other boy. "I was meeting some of our neighbors, Stain."

I frowned. *His name was* Stain?

The boy wandered over to us. "Hi," he said. "I'm Frankie Castillo. I see you've met my lazy big brother already."

I almost laughed at myself for not realizing right away that *stain* had been a big-brother insult.

"I'm Emma," I said, "and this is Hallie, and Annie. Oh, and Cupid. Welcome to Highbury!"

I think Frankie rolled his eyes a little as he said, "Thanks."

"What grade are you in?" I asked him.

"Seventh," he said. "I know I look old for my age."

Mateo groaned out loud. "We know you *sound* stupid for your age," he said to Frankie, then turned to the rest of us. "I apologize for the human stain otherwise known as my brother."

Mateo had been so nice and polite . . . until his little brother came along. At that moment, I was pretty glad to be an only child, or at least *not* to be anybody's younger sister.

"We're in seventh too," Hallie told Frankie, and he shrugged. I bristled. He didn't seem very nice.

"Boys, where are you?" a woman's voice called from the garage. "Your dad and I need your help!"

"Coming!" Frankie called in the direction of the garage. "See ya at school," he told me and Hallie, before racing back toward his house.

"I should go too," Mateo said, but he looked *very* reluctant to leave Annie's side.

"I could come over and help," Annie offered with a shy smile. "Except I promised these two . . ." She glanced apologetically at me and Hallie.

"It's okay!" both Hallie and I said at the same time.

"We can meet up another day," I added.

"Let me just go tell my mom where I'll be," Annie told Mateo. She waved goodbye to me and Hallie, knelt down to give Cupid a quick kiss on the top of his head, and ran back toward her house. Mateo watched her go with a dreamy smile on his face. He didn't even notice when Hallie and I said goodbye to him and walked off with Cupid trotting along between us.

I turned to Hallie. "I'm sorry Annie bailed on the cheer squad prep," I said.

"It's really fine," Hallie said, and for the first time that day, she was smiling. "I actually told my mom I'd help her with some chores around the house today, so it works out better this way."

"Are you sure you're okay with it?" I asked. "I can see if Annie would meet us tomorrow . . ."

Hallie shook her head. "No, Emma. Really." She took a deep breath and added, "I decided I'm not going to try out for the cheer squad."

My stomach dropped. I'd been talking Hallie into trying out for the cheer squad since *last* year. I just knew she'd be great at it. "Wait, what?" I said. "Now I feel terrible! I shouldn't have suggested—"

"No, Emma, look—you're not listening to me, okay?" Hallie said, sounding frustrated. "I was seriously wavering on the whole idea anyway, and I'm taking this as a sign. I feel really . . . relieved now that I've decided not to do it. So, that should tell you something."

"Oh. Okay." I tried not to let my disappointment show on my face. I thought I was being helpful, encouraging Hallie to try out. "You'd be amazing, though . . . I mean, you're such a good dancer."

We turned onto my street, with Cupid stopping occasionally to sniff at a tree root.

"Thanks," Hallie said. "But I think I'm more of a freestyler than a choreo girl. I'll still get a chance to tear it up at the dance next month." She shot me a grin.

"Yeah, you will!" I said, newly excited. Next month was the Valentine's Day dance at school, something Hallie and I had both been looking forward to. We'd gone together last year, and it had been a blast.

"I was even wondering," Hallie added, and her cheeks turned pink—but not from the cold. "If we might end up bringing dates this year? I heard from Autumn Hawkins that in seventh grade it's practically a *requirement* to have a date to the Valentine's dance."

"Really?" I said, surprised. I hadn't thought about *that* part of the dance. I bit my lip. Who could Hallie and I take as dates? We definitely didn't have boyfriends.

But thinking about dates reminded me of Annie and Mateo, and I turned to Hallie with a smile. "Can you believe what happened with Annie and that new boy?" I asked. "It was just so amazing how Cupid—"

"Set them up? Yeah, I caught that too." Hallie laughed.

I picked Cupid up and put his little wrinkly face close to mine. "You're a wonder pup, yes, you are! I must have had a premonition when I named you Cupid. You're basically a matchmaker."

We had reached my house, so Hallie gave me a hug and rubbed Cupid's head before turning to go back to her house.

Now, sitting in my bedroom with Cupid in my lap, a few hours after the Annie/Mateo meet-cute, I thought back to how my pug had gotten his name. My dad is a professor of ethics and philosophy at a small college in the neighboring town. He's a huge fan of everything from the classical period, so I grew up learning all about Plato, Aristotle, and Socrates—but also all about the ancient gods and goddesses like Mars, Cupid, and Venus. When I finally talked my father into letting me have a dog for my tenth birthday, Cupid seemed like the perfect name. After all, one look into his big, round brown eyes and I felt like I'd been hit with one of the love god's arrows. From the first moment I saw him, I loved that pug more than words could ever say.

Forgetting about my journal entry for the moment, I

scratched Cupid under his chin. "You're the best matchmaking pug in the whole world," I told him. I didn't actually *know* of any other matchmaking pugs in the world, so it seemed a safe bet. "The best!"

"You are going to give that little dog a very big ego," said a voice from the doorway, and I jumped in surprise.

2

Finally, Theo

"Oh, Dad—I didn't see you there!" I said. I stood up from my desk, scooping Cupid into my arms.

Dad didn't usually surprise me—he was too tall to do much sneaking around. He was skinny, and his kind expression meant no one was ever intimidated by him. As usual, his dark hair was sticking in all directions because he was constantly running his hands through it.

"I'm sorry I startled you, sweetie," Dad said. "I came up to tell you that Theo is here. His family just got back from their trip."

"Finally!" I said. "I still can't believe he missed New Year's!"

But Dad didn't respond because I was already rushing past him and heading downstairs, Cupid at my heels.

Theo and I had been friends ever since he moved to the neighborhood when I was in first grade. His parents are both archaeologists, so they often travel all over the world with Theo in tow. They were supposed to be back yesterday, in time for the neighborhood New Year's party, which Dad and I had hosted this year.

"Where are you?" I called when I reached the bottom of the stairway and didn't see Theo in his customary spot in our living room.

"Kitchen," Theo said, and I rounded the corner to find Theo leaning against the counter. His dark brown hair was in need of a cut; it swooped low over his green eyes.

"*Finally* you make it downstairs," Theo said. He put down the sandwich he'd already somehow made to kneel and pet Cupid, whose little tail was wagging with joy. I sighed. When you have an utterly adorable dog, you get used to being greeted second.

"Nice to see you too," I said as I watched Cupid enthusiastically lick Theo's face.

"I missed good old American sandwiches," Theo said, standing up and taking a huge bite of the one he'd made.

"Well, we missed *you* at the party last night," I said. Cupid trotted back over to me and I lifted him into my arms so he could lick my cheek.

"Ourfly waz drayed."

"Maybe you should finish chewing before you talk," I told Theo.

He swallowed the giant bite. "Our flight was delayed. And we were at this really small airport in western Egypt. There were no places to get food, and we were afraid to leave the airport in case our flight was called."

"You guys stopped for food somewhere on the way home, though?"

Theo swallowed another big bite. "Yeah, but I was still hungry."

"Of course," I said with a laugh. I sat down on one of our

kitchen barstools as Theo resumed eating his sandwich. I set Cupid down, and he curled up around the stool's legs.

"So how was the party?" Theo asked. "What did you and Cupid wear? Did you do an outfit change halfway through like you were hosting the Oscars?"

I rolled my eyes. "I wore *one* very nice sparkly black dress, thank you very much. And Cupid looked smashing in his matching suit. Didn't you, boy?"

Cupid barked in agreement.

"You get through the hosting duties without having a meltdown?" Theo asked, taking a big swig from the can of sparkling water he'd also found in our fridge.

"What do you mean?" I said huffily. "It was just the neighborhood party. We have the same food and games every year." Theo was one whole year older than me, a fact he never failed to bring up on an almost-daily basis. And he liked to act "older and wiser" whenever he had the chance.

"I know, but you do get kind of intense when it comes to planning events," Theo said with a mischievous smile.

I watched him polish off one of the three pickles he'd chosen to go with his second dinner. "I do not 'get intense,'" I told him. "Anyway, you missed the entire event, so you don't get to say anything about it."

"I'm sorry, Em. I wanted to be there. I know I missed our annual trivia game."

I shrugged and tore off a paper towel to pass to him.

"I should get out of here," Theo said as he finished his sandwich in two big bites. "I have a ton of homework to do. Although I forgot to bring my science book and my math notebook home from school before my trip."

I cleared my throat and pointed at the other end of the counter, where a neat pile of Theo's schoolbooks was stacked.

"You got my stuff out of my locker? Thanks, Emma! Wait, why do you have my combination?"

"Who do you think put the spirit boxes in your locker during basketball season?" I asked, crossing my arms.

"Always looking out for me. Even if you have to snoop to do it. Hey," he said. I'd been putting the lid back on the mayo jar, but the change in his tone made me look up. I sometimes forgot just how green his eyes were. He was lucky—they looked even greener because of the contrast with his dark hair.

"I really am sorry we didn't get to play our New Year's trivia game."

Why did Theo sound so serious all of a sudden? I waved a hand in the air. "It's fine. You'll make it up to me by volunteering at the winter carnival."

I stuck the mayo in the fridge and turned to see Theo staring at me, realization dawning on his face. "*Em-ma*. You don't mean the dunk tank. I've told you before . . ."

"It's for charity, Theo," I reminded him.

"Theo, would you like me to make you something to eat?" Dad appeared in the kitchen doorway, and I jumped again. "Sorry, Em," Dad said, seeing that he'd startled me *again*.

"He's already made himself a sandwich," I told Dad.

"Yeah, hope you don't mind, Mr. Winters," Theo said.

"Of course not, Theo. Did Emma give you your school things?"

"She did. What would I do without Emma?"

"I don't know what I would do myself, Theo," Dad said. Now *he* sounded serious. What was with everyone today?

Cupid gave a bark as though he were agreeing with Dad,

and then all three of us laughed. Theo waved goodbye before heading home.

I carried Cupid upstairs. He has very short legs, so I try not to let him use the stairs too much—I don't want him to hurt his tiny back. When I got to my room, I changed into my pajamas and sat down at the little vanity table that had been my mother's. It was another of those old-fashioned things I liked so much. Although I didn't really wear makeup yet, I still liked to sit in the small chair like Mom used to, staring into the same mirror. I always wondered if I looked like her. My mom had died when I was so young, three and a half, that I didn't really remember her. Of course, I'd seen lots of pictures. It was clear that we had the same auburn hair, pale skin, and light hazel eyes. But it was hard to tell from a picture whether we truly were alike.

What I mostly wondered, as always, was whether or not she would be proud of me. I liked to think that she would. But there was no way that I could ever really be sure.

I pulled out my journal and, at the top of a fresh page, wrote the question that was chasing around in my head: What would Mom think if she could meet me now?

Usually, I loved to write. It helped me gather my thoughts together. But now I couldn't think of what else to say. I swallowed past a sudden lump in my throat and closed the journal. Then I said good night to Cupid and turned out the light.

3

Unwelcome Wagon

The walk from my house to school is only about five minutes. But on that first day back after winter break, I walked slowly, appreciating the satisfying crunch of frost-covered leaves beneath my feet. Besides, school didn't start for another hour, so I had lots of time.

I knew Ms. Bates would be in the library when I got there. Ms. Bates is the school librarian, and also the advisor of SAC, the student activities committee. I hoped she had time to go over some of my ideas for the winter carnival and the Valentine's dance.

Ms. Bates is one of the smartest people I know, which is

saying something, considering that I know my father and both of Theo's parents. Ms. Bates seems to collect misfortunes, though. She is always dealing with some catastrophe or other. When I reached the library, it was clear what today's problem was: The temperature inside had to be at least ninety degrees.

I found Ms. Bates standing on a chair, peering up at the ceiling. "Oh, Emma!" she said when she turned around and saw me. "The heat's been blasting all night, and I don't know how to shut it off! And Mr. Carver won't be in for another hour—I've already checked."

Mr. Carver was sort of the Hagrid of our school—the one who had all the keys and fixed everything. I walked closer to where Ms. Bates stood. Her light brown hair was escaping from her ponytail, making her look frazzled.

"Why don't you come down?" I called up to her. I didn't want to say it out loud, but I was kind of afraid she would fall.

"Well, there are pipes up here," she told me with a shrug. "I've looked everywhere else."

"Maybe take off your sweater?" I suggested gently. Poor Ms.

Bates's face was red and glistening with sweat, but she still wore the Ravenclaw cardigan I'd gotten her for Christmas.

"Oh!" She looked down at herself, as though surprised she had the sweater on. "Good point, Emma. Thank you!" She hopped down off the chair and tugged off her sweater. "What are you doing in so early?" she asked me as she smoothed down her white blouse.

I held up my notebook. "Well, I had some ideas for things we should lock down for the carnival. But they can wait until your sauna is fixed."

"No, no!" Ms. Bates exclaimed. "Let's start talking now." She collapsed into her creaky office chair with a sigh. "Everything in this old town is always breaking! Between you and me, Emma? It would be nice to head out of town once in a while."

Personally, I didn't understand why *anyone* would ever want to leave Highbury, but Ms. Bates had been wishing she wasn't stuck here for as long as I could remember. In her heart of hearts, I knew she always really wanted to go to New York City and work in a library or a bookstore there. If she lived in such an exciting place, Ms. Bates often said, she could finally start that novel she'd always wanted to write. She'd told me about it in September while I'd helped her plan the fall carnival.

I would really miss her if she ever left. Ms. Bates was one of my favorite adults.

The phone on her desk rang, and after she said hello and listened for just a few seconds, I heard her say, "Oh, thank goodness! See you soon.

"Mr. Carver's coming in early," she told me. She sat back in her chair again, fanning herself with a manila folder. I felt a small shudder at the state of the folder—she'd crossed out the label on the little notch at least twice and written over it, and the edges were all bent and crinkly. Just looking at it was stressing me out.

"What if we met up after school instead?" I asked her. Dad only had morning classes on Thursdays, so he could walk Cupid if I stayed late at school.

"Sounds like a plan. I'm going to head to the faculty lounge to get some coffee. *Iced* coffee," she added dramatically, and I had to giggle as I followed her out of the library and into the much-cooler hallway.

The school was still pretty empty as I walked to my locker—just a few tired-looking teachers headed for the coffee machine like Ms. Bates. I thought about what else I could get accomplished now that my main mission for the morning hadn't worked out.

Then it hit me: Annie's new neighbor, Frankie, had said, "See ya at school." He must have been starting today. It wasn't much notice, but I could get Mrs. Kruger in the front office to help me pull together a new-student welcome basket. We didn't get very many new kids, so it was tradition to provide them with a basket, and a "buddy" to be their tour guide for the first day.

I wondered who would be a good buddy for Frankie and immediately thought of Theo. Even though Theo was a grade ahead, he would be the perfect person to show Frankie around and introduce him to people. Everybody likes Theo.

I rounded the corner and almost ran into Theo himself.

"Hey, Em," he said with a smile. "What are you doing here? This is early even for you."

"I was gonna meet with Ms. Bates, but the library was on fire."

"What?" he asked, his eyes wide with alarm.

I pulled on his arm to stop him racing off toward the library. "Not *literally*. The heat is stuck on—it was running all night and it was super hot in there. Ms. Bates said we could meet after school instead. Anyway, what are *you* doing here so early? You usually like to slide in two minutes before the late bell."

Theo laughed. "I was hoping to make up my math test, but Ms. Marshall's not here yet."

"Well, I'm going to the front office. I forgot to tell you yesterday: Hallie and I met two new kids moving in next door to Annie Taylor. Mateo is a senior, but his younger brother Frankie's coming here to start in seventh. I thought maybe you could show him around?"

"Sure," Theo said, and we headed off together toward the front office.

"Good morning, Mrs. Kruger," we said in unison as we entered.

"Good morning to you, Emma! And welcome back, Theo!" Mrs. Kruger beamed at us. Even though everyone likes Theo, adults *love* him. But Mrs. Kruger also loved me; I was willing to bet that I was one of the only students who ever asked her about her cat, who had a problem with hair balls.

"Mrs. K, did you hear about a new student starting today?" I asked now.

"We got a phone call just before the holiday break," she said, opening a folder beside her computer. I had to admire Mrs. Kruger's organizational system. Her folders were all labeled perfectly. "Frankie Elias Castillo. Grade seven," she read out loud, and then looked up at me. "How did you know?"

"I met him yesterday. He moved next door to Annie Taylor."

"Oh, I remember Annie Taylor. Such a sweet girl! Is she still cheerleading?"

"Captain of the squad," I answered. I didn't tell her that I hoped she and Frankie Castillo's handsome big brother were already hitting it off, thanks to my little Cupid. "I was hoping we could pull together some welcome stuff for Frankie. Like an HMS T-shirt, and maybe some other spirit stuff? And Theo said he'd be his buddy, unless you've got someone else picked out."

"That's a very sweet idea," Mrs. K said. "I think all of that stuff's locked in Vice Principal Jericho's office closet, so we'll have to wait until she gets here. And I don't see a buddy assignment anywhere in the file. It's so nice of you both to help a new student get settled. So, Theo, where were you visiting this time?"

"Morocco and Egypt," Theo answered. "Both were amazing! It's nice to be home, though."

"I'm sure it is. There's no place like Highbury." I smiled at Mrs. K, since I agreed completely about our town.

Just then, the bell on the top of the office door dinged, and in walked a short, pretty woman with light brown skin and dark hair. Behind her, walking with his head down, was Frankie Castillo.

"This must be Frankie!" Mrs. Kruger exclaimed. "We were

just getting everything ready for you. I have your schedule and such right here."

"Thank you." The woman smiled at Mrs. K. "I'm Aitana Castillo, and this is indeed my son Frankie." She leaned in a bit closer to Mrs. Kruger and said in a lower voice, "He's not very happy to be here, I'm afraid. I apologize in advance for any surliness."

"I understand completely," Mrs. K said. "It's hard to change schools. But, Frankie, I have your buddy standing right here. This is Theo Knight. He's one of our top students. And I hear you've already met Emma Winters."

"Yeah," Frankie grunted, reaching up and taking the schedule Mrs. K held out to him.

Mrs. Kruger was peering down at her computer. "It looks like you've got history with Mr. Turner first period."

"I had him last year," Theo said cheerfully. "He's really nice. Frankie, you can come with me and I'll show you where the room is."

"Okay," Frankie said, although he didn't sound very excited about it.

"Your mother will take care of your paperwork, Frankie," Mrs. K explained. "You go start getting the lay of the land with Theo and Emma."

Mrs. Castillo gave a grateful smile to Theo and me.

"Thanks, Mrs. K," I said. "I'll come back at lunch for those *things* we were talking about?" She nodded. "Oh, and I hope Waffles is doing better now that she's on that new medicine."

"She is! Thank you so much for asking," Mrs. K said, then gave us a happy wave as Theo, Frankie, and I headed out of the office.

"She has a kid named Waffles?" Frankie asked.

Theo snorted. "I wish. I think it's her cat, though, right, Emma?"

"Waffles is a cat," I answered with a nod.

Frankie let out a small grunt. Theo opened the door to the stairwell, and Frankie walked through without looking back at us. Theo raised an eyebrow at me, but he followed Frankie and let the door swing shut.

Frankie definitely didn't seem very happy to be here in Highbury. I hoped his brother was having a better time of it at the high school, with Annie as his tour guide.

At lunchtime, as planned, I went back to the front office to pick up the spirit stuff. Mrs. Kruger had gone above and beyond, putting everything in a basket and tying it with black-and-gold ribbon to match our school colors. The basket was heavy to carry along with my backpack, but I made it to the cafeteria huffing and puffing.

The cafeteria was already loud and packed with students. All the grades eat together because our school is so small. I spotted Theo first, sitting with his friends from his grade. Sometimes Theo ate with those friends, and sometimes he sat with me and Hallie for lunch. He floated easily between groups.

Today, I figured Frankie would probably be sitting beside him. But Theo caught my eye and shrugged; I followed the direction of his gaze and saw Frankie sitting off at a table by himself.

The sight made me feel sad, but then again, I could tell from Theo's shrug that he'd tried to invite Frankie to sit with him and his friends.

I marched over to where Frankie was picking at a sad slice of pizza and plopped the basket down in front of his lunch tray.

"Welcome to HMS!" I said.

Frankie frowned, glancing first at me and then the basket warily. "I don't need any of that."

I blinked in surprise. "Oh." I stared down at the basket. Did he mean he wanted me to take it back? I wasn't sure what reaction I'd been expecting, but this definitely wasn't it.

"Look, it's really nice of you and all," Frankie said. "But I've moved schools before, and I'm kind of over all this welcome-wagon crap. No offense."

I was plenty offended, but I wasn't going to give Frankie the satisfaction of showing it. "Fine by me," I said coolly, but I left the basket sitting where it was. I certainly wasn't going to take it back after I'd carried it all the way here.

Before I could lose my temper and snap at Frankie, Hallie came up behind me with her tray. She pushed the basket aside and sat down opposite Frankie. "I know, changing schools sucks," she said.

I stood frozen, feeling awkward. Was Hallie taking Frankie's side?

"But Emma's just trying to make you feel welcome here," she

continued, and I felt myself relax. Of course Hallie would have my back. I sat down beside her. Without even looking over at me, Hallie handed me half her turkey sub, and I took a bite. "When I started new in fourth, my mom forgot to send me with a lunch or lunch money. Emma gave me *her* lunch, then marched back up to the cafeteria line and charmed another meal out of the lunch lady."

Frankie smiled. It wasn't a huge smile, but it was a smile. I looked over at Hallie with a grateful smile of my own.

I thought about how maybe Frankie had a best friend, like I had Hallie, and had to leave them behind to move here. If that were true, it was no wonder a basket full of Highbury Hornets stuff wasn't going to magically fix all that.

"So, you guys are the Hornets?" Frankie asked.

I nodded. "The high school teams are the Tigers, but somebody decided to go for alliteration with the middle school mascot."

"It could be worse," Frankie said. "At my old middle school we were the Ducklings."

"I'm sure the other teams were petrified," Hallie said with a straight face. I giggled.

Frankie snorted. "Yeah. Terrified."

"Did you play any sports at your old school?" Hallie asked Frankie.

"Just soccer."

"Soccer tryouts are next week here," I told him. I wasn't very athletically inclined myself, but I did keep track of the sports seasons as part of the Spirit Club. Theo played soccer, and I always made sure I got his name to make his spirit boxes. No one else knew all his favorite cookies and snacks like I did.

"Cool. I'll probably try out," Frankie said.

"I'm going to go to Morning Mugs on the way home, get a milkshake or something. You want to come?" Hallie was asking both of us.

"I have to meet Ms. Bates right after school, but I could come after."

"Sounds good," Frankie said.

I looked over at Hallie. Her low-maintenance approach to welcoming Frankie had definitely worked out way better than my giant-basket method had.

I took the last bite of my half of the sub and tried not to let that bother me too much.

I stepped into the bright, cozy interior of Morning Mugs and breathed in the smell of their yummy hot cocoa. I expected Frankie and Hallie to already be there, but there were only a couple of adults sitting at the little round tables.

"Hi, Emma," Stella greeted me from behind the counter. She and her sister Shana had owned Morning Mugs forever. "And, Abby, hi!" she added as Ms. Bates stepped in behind me.

When I'd told Ms. Bates about Frankie, and how Hallie had invited him here, she'd suggested we could have our meeting at the coffee shop as easily as in the library. Besides, it was still pretty hot in there, even after Mr. Carver had fixed the thermostat.

"I just had to get out of that library, Stella," Ms. Bates was saying as we followed Stella to a corner table. "No hot tea for me today. Put my usual on ice, please."

"Sure thing, Abby."

Stella didn't have to ask me for my order. I'm a creature of habit, and since she and Shana let me bring Cupid in with me, I'm kind of a regular. In the winter, I always order their delicious peppermint cocoa.

The bell on the café door jangled, and Theo walked in, with Hallie and Frankie right behind him.

"We took Frankie to meet Coach Karlin," Hallie told me as they came over. That was a good idea—introducing him to the soccer coach.

"Frankie, this is Ms. Bates—our school librarian," I said. "She's also the head of our activities committee, and we were going to go over some plans for the winter carnival."

Ms. Bates stood up. "We can do that later, Emma. I won't interrupt you getting to know your new friend. See if you can convince any of these wonderful kids to be part of the dunk tank, and I'll go have my tea and catch up with Stella."

Before I could say anything else, Ms. Bates had made her way over to one of the stools at the café's counter. Frankie, Hallie, and Theo pulled up chairs and joined me at the table.

When Stella came over with my mug of cocoa, her jaw dropped. "Theo!" she exclaimed. "I think you grew a foot while you were away!"

Theo turned a little pink, but I realized that Stella was right. Theo *had* gotten taller in the last month or so.

"I'll have a cocoa too, but just the plain kind," he said when Stella asked for everyone's orders.

"I'll have a chocolate milkshake," Hallie said.

"Make that two," Frankie added.

Stella nodded and headed back to the kitchen. As I took a sip of my cocoa, my phone buzzed. It was a text from Dad, asking if I wanted him to bring Cupid over to Morning Mugs. Then we could all go get sandwiches for dinner at The Elephant afterward. I texted back a thumbs-up. Dad likes to eat dinner *very* early. It's better for the digestion, he says.

"What was your season like last year?" Frankie was asking Theo, and I felt myself begin to tune out the way I often did whenever the subject of sports—especially sports stats—came up.

Theo said some numbers, Frankie gave one of his grunts, and then Stella came back with everyone's drinks. As Hallie and Frankie sipped their milkshakes and Theo drank his cocoa, I took another sip from my own mug.

"So, any takers for that dunk tank idea Ms. Bates mentioned?" I asked. "It's always our biggest moneymaker."

"I've already told you no like a thousand times," Theo said, though he smiled as he said it. "I'll literally make a donation instead. Besides, *you're* not doing it."

"I'm *planning* the event," I said. "Besides, you know my dad would never let me get in that tank."

"Emma's dad's kind of a germophobe," Hallie told Frankie.

"He's not!" I protested. "He's just . . . very conscientious about health."

Then, as though I'd magically made him appear with my words, Dad walked into the café with Cupid on his leash.

And for the second time in two days, Cupid began barking excitedly and pulled so hard on his leash that Dad had to let go. But instead of running for me, as I would have expected, he made a beeline for Ms. Bates.

I stood up and rushed to Cupid, but Ms. Bates had already crouched down and was receiving a bunch of very wet pug kisses. Her giggle made her sound happier than I'd ever heard her.

Dad apologized and knelt down to pick up Cupid. My little pug squirmed around happily, and planted one giant, definitely germy, absolutely sweet pug kiss on my dad—right on his mouth.

With a glare, Dad handed Cupid back to me and wiped his face with his jacket sleeve.

"I'm so sorry," Dad said again to Ms. Bates. "Cupid has never done that! I assure you, that dog was put through lots of training when he was a puppy. But I'm afraid my daughter and Theo encourage that . . . unsanitary habit." He pulled one of his handkerchiefs out of his jacket pocket—Dad likes old-fashioned things too, which is probably where I get it—and Ms. Bates accepted it, blotting at her face where Cupid had slobbered.

"It's no problem," Ms. Bates said to Dad with a big smile.

I froze. Something in her voice and expression made me realize: Cupid had just done it again.

Except this time, it seemed like Cupid had chosen a match for *my dad*.

4

Cupid Strikes Again

I stood there in shock, still holding a very wriggly matchmaking dog.

Ms. Bates was gazing at my dad, her eyes sparkling.

And Dad, well, his face had gotten sort of red, and he was doing that nervous cough thing he always did when he didn't know what to say.

Yesterday, when Cupid had matched Annie and Mateo, *I* had jumped in and helped things along.

But now my mouth felt much too dry. Even swallowing seemed difficult.

I thought about how lonely Dad sometimes seemed. Like the night over winter break when Hallie and I had gone to Autumn Hawkins's party, and he had stayed home alone. Maybe I should say something . . . continue what Cupid had started.

But Hallie had already jumped in for me. "Ms. Bates is having a heck of a day," she told my dad. Then she glanced at Ms. Bates. "You should tell Mr. Winters about what happened in the library, Ms. Bates."

My dad smiled. "Ah, Ms. Bates! I'm glad we're finally meeting. Emma speaks so fondly of you."

Was *Ms. Bates* blushing? "Likewise," she said. "Emma and I were going to work in the library together, but like Hallie said, we had a minor crisis. The heat was on all night! And it took several hours to fix this morning. I confess it still has me a bit rattled."

"That's terrible!" my dad said sympathetically. "Coming in from the cold outside to such a blast of heat—it really can't be good for you."

Ms. Bates was frowning now, maybe worrying about something she hadn't been before.

"I'm sorry," Dad said. "I didn't mean to concern you. I guess I'm just an old valetudinarian."

Ms. Bates's frown vanished, and she smiled again. "I doubt that! Besides, I can be a bit of a hypochondriac myself!"

That sealed it—here were the only two people in the world who knew what valetude-whatever meant. I couldn't get in the way of that.

"A cold dinner could be just the thing after a day in the hot library?" I suggested. I glanced at Dad. "Maybe Ms. Bates could come with us to The Elephant to get one of their yummy sandwiches?"

Theo caught my eye and smiled at me, so I knew I must be on the right track.

"Or Emma could come to dinner with us?" he asked. "If you don't mind, Mr. Winters. We're showing a new kid around town. Frankie just moved here yesterday." Theo gestured at Frankie, who gave the kind of wave you'd expect from somebody who usually said yes by grunting.

"I suppose that could work," Dad said. "If that's okay with you, Ms. Bates?"

"Please, call me Abby."

And just like that my dad had a date.

As Dad and Ms. Bates chatted some more, I joined Theo and Hallie back at the table where Frankie was slurping up the last of his milkshake. I was still more than a little bit in shock. I sat down again and settled Cupid in my lap. He was less wriggly now.

"We're taking you to dinner," Theo told Frankie. "If you want. There's a diner just a block away."

"Okay," Frankie said. "I just have to text my mom." He looked over at me. "Cute dog."

"Thanks. Do you want to pet him?"

Frankie nodded and moved over to sit beside me, petting Cupid's head. "We had a Yorkie when I was younger. I miss that dog."

"Well, you can share Cupid," I told him. Frankie looked up at me, and I was surprised to see what seemed like a real smile on his face.

"It's good you like dogs, because if you hang around Emma, you'll be seeing a *lot* of Cupid. He's spoiled rotten," Theo said.

"He is not!" I argued.

Hallie gave a pointed cough. "Um, say that when he's riding around in his custom-made stroller."

"And the only reason he's not wearing an outfit today is because your dad brought him over here," Theo chimed in.

I pulled my pug closer and kissed the top of his furry head. "Don't listen to them, Cupid. They just don't understand."

Dad came over to the table then, Ms. Bates beside him. "We're going to head over to The Elephant," he told me, even though I'd been there when they'd made the plan two minutes ago. His hair was even wilder than usual, but his eyes were crinkly at the corners—he looked happy. "Does that sound all right?"

"Of course," I said, wondering why he was asking me again. "We're going to The Dinner Bell, and then I'll be home."

"Do you want to take Cupid home first?" Dad asked.

"He can come to the diner. Mario will let him in if we eat in the back room," I answered.

"Okay," Dad said. "Um, have fun, kids," he added, sounding even more awkward than usual.

Ms. Bates waved to us all, and I watched as the two of them left Morning Mugs together.

"Are they . . . going on a date?" Frankie asked.

"I think so," I said. "I really do think so."

"That's so cute!" Hallie exclaimed.

"That was a nice thing you did there," Theo said in a low voice.

I nodded. I didn't remind him it was Hallie who'd started it.

"Everybody ready for some grilled cheese and fries?" I asked, changing the subject. I stood up and set Cupid on the floor. His tail wagged as he sniffed around for crumbs.

"You don't have to order grilled cheese and fries," Hallie explained to Frankie as they got up from the table. "That's just what Emma always gets."

"It's the best thing on the menu," I told Frankie, "but of course you're free to order something else."

Hallie and Theo laughed. Frankie looked at me again; this time it seemed like he was trying to figure me out.

With Cupid on his leash, Theo, Frankie, Hallie, and I left Morning Mugs and set out for The Dinner Bell. As we walked, I wondered what my dad and Ms. Bates were talking about right now.

*   *   *

We all ended up ordering grilled cheese and fries for dinner, and everyone agreed that it was, in fact, a delicious meal. When we were done, Hallie texted her mom to come pick her up; Hallie lives farther away from downtown than I do. Frankie caught a ride with them, and Theo walked back home with me and Cupid.

"You're pretty quiet," he said as we started down the sidewalk. "And you only ate half your grilled cheese."

"You ate the other half, so it didn't go to waste," I said, wrapping my scarf tighter around my neck.

"Well, Cupid had a big bite of it too," Theo pointed out. He paused, then asked, "Are you worried about your dad and Ms. Bates?"

I stopped to let Cupid do his business under a tree. "I'm not *worried*," I tried to explain. "It's just . . . it seems . . . weird. I feel . . . weird about it."

"So, *weird*, then?" Theo asked. It was getting dark, but I could hear the smile in his voice.

"Don't make fun of me."

"I'm not. Emma, I think it's totally normal for you to

feel . . . uncertain about your dad dating again. But I gotta say, I think this could be really great for him. If it works out, I mean."

"Yeah," I said as we continued walking.

"But you know," Theo added. "They just went to get sandwiches, after all. It's not like they're getting married . . ."

"Getting *married*!" I stopped walking and turned to him. "Why would you even say that? They were . . . and Cupid just . . . and they're just eating sandwiches!" I finished.

Theo put a hand on my arm. "Em, I said they're *not* . . . look, would it even be so bad if eventually they did? You love Ms. Bates."

We'd reached a streetlight, and I looked into Theo's green eyes. He really was taller now. I realized Theo was right. I did love Ms. Bates. Maybe Cupid's magic really had struck again. And Dad and Ms. Bates were sort of perfect for each other if I let myself admit it.

But then I thought of Ms. Bates moving into our *house*, and I started to feel really weird again.

"Just promise me that if it does happen it'll take a really, really long time?" I didn't know why I was asking Theo to promise that. It wasn't like he was actually in charge of my dad's life. But Theo nodded anyway. "I promise. Remember how long it took your dad to pick out a new car last year?"

I smiled, thinking about the months and months of research. My father was not exactly Mr. Spontaneous.

When we reached my house, Theo walked me in to say hi to my dad. I knew he was just making sure Dad's date was over and the coast was clear before he left me.

"See you in the morning, Em," Theo called after he waved to Dad.

"How was The Elephant?" I asked Dad as I got out some kibble for Cupid. Mario, the owner of The Dinner Bell, had given Cupid a bunch of snacks, but my pup was overdue for his real dinner.

"It was very nice," Dad answered, sitting down at the kitchen table. "I like Abby a lot. I knew you enjoyed having her as the advisor of student activities, but I suppose I didn't expect to have so much in common with her. Did you know she was a classics major in college?"

"Along with English lit," I told him. Suddenly, it seemed

important for him to know that I knew more about Ms. Bates than he did.

I studied Dad. He was sitting in his usual chair, wearing his favorite slippers, just like always. But he looked happier, somehow—younger, even.

So I said, "I'm glad you had fun." And I kissed him on the cheek before heading upstairs with Cupid to do my homework.

And silently, I vowed to try to feel less *weird* about my pug's latest match.

5

Maybe . . .

The next day, I ran into Frankie as I was walking to school. Frankie was quiet as usual, but I had some ideas for him.

"I know you'll be busy with soccer," I said as we walked along, "but I can introduce you to everyone on the student activities committee, in case you'd like to sign up for other things."

"Okay," he said, although he didn't sound excited. I decided not to let his lack of enthusiasm slow me down. I was going to make Frankie feel welcome at HMS whether he liked it or not.

When we got to school, Frankie looked around in surprise at the nearly empty hallways.

"We're here really early, aren't we?" he asked me. "My mom told me to give myself enough time to get to school, but I didn't realize how short the walk was."

"Yeah," I said. "But I always get to school early. On purpose."

Frankie snorted. "Why?"

I shrugged, feeling defensive. "Because I do. *You* don't have to, though . . ."

Frankie laughed. "Sorry. I didn't mean it like that. I'm just messing with you, Emma."

"Oh. Okay." Something about Frankie always had me off balance.

Frankie and I headed over to our lockers—they were in the same row. I was hanging up my jacket when Theo appeared beside us.

"I guess you walked to school with Emma," Theo told Frankie. "Going to challenge her title for student who gets to school first?"

"No way. Besides, aren't *you* here early too?" Frankie pointed out.

Theo grinned. "You got me there. But I missed three and

a half weeks of school before break, so I've got a lot of makeup tests and quizzes."

"Where'd you go?" Frankie asked, and when Theo told him he'd been to Morocco and Egypt, Frankie's eyes widened.

"Seriously?" Frankie said. "That's so cool. I've never been out of the country. Well, just Canada."

"Canada's great. Where did you go?" Theo leaned against the lockers. With a sigh, I reorganized the already-organized top shelf of my locker.

"Toronto."

"Someday you've got to go to Quebec—it's such an interesting place . . ."

Frankie nodded along, looking much more interested than he usually did.

Great. Yet another person who'd been bitten by the travel bug and was impressed with *all* the places Theo had been. Why couldn't people just appreciate good old Highbury?

"I actually brought back some stuff from the trip to show Mr. Denton, my history teacher," Theo said. "I'm headed there now if you want to come see?"

"Sure," Frankie said. "See you later, Emma?" he called as they turned to walk off together.

I nodded. "Yep, see you in English."

"Bye, Em," Theo called.

"Having trouble hogging the new boy while Theo's around?" a voice asked in my ear.

I jumped and spun to see Autumn Hawkins standing beside me with her usual smirk on her face.

Technically, Autumn is my friend. I've known her all my life. We're in the same grade, and she's my co-chair for our grade in SAC. We have all the same friends, and I've been to her house more times than I can count. But she also really bugs me a lot of the time. With Autumn, it's like everything is a competition, and I'm the person she's always out to beat.

"I'm not *hogging* him," I said. "Besides, of course Frankie wants to hang out with Theo. He's *Theo*."

Autumn rolled her eyes. "And we all know how big of a Theo fan *you* are."

I frowned. "What's that supposed to mean?"

"Nothing. Anyway, come on, emergency SAC meeting."

"What? I didn't get a text."

"I totally texted you last night. You must not have checked." Autumn pulled her phone from her pocket.

I knew we were rivals sometimes, but would Autumn actually go so far as to *not* tell me about a meeting just so I might miss it?

"Oh no," she said, "it didn't go through, see?"

I saw a red exclamation point beside her last message, and there was my name at the top of her phone screen. So at least I knew she was telling the truth. I followed her to the library.

"Good, you two are here!" Ms. Bates called as soon as we walked in.

I looked around and saw that there were kids from the SAC team seated at the library tables. Autumn and I took seats at a free table while Ms. Bates faced us at the front of the room. I tried not to think about her date with Dad last night.

"We've got a problem, folks," Ms. Bates announced. "I've just been told that our winter carnival date conflicts with a speaker the parent organization hired to come to school. If we still want to hold the carnival, it will need to happen soon."

"Really?" Amy Marston, one of the eighth-grade chairs, crossed her arms and frowned.

I tried not to frown at *her*. What did Amy care? She'd been elected because she was popular, but she never actually did any work.

I raised my hand. "What do you mean when you say *soon*?" I asked.

"Soon as in next Saturday," Ms. Bates replied briskly. "It's the only date that works with the school's calendar."

My mouth dropped open. *Next* Saturday?

"Ugh, no one comes when it's a Saturday. We tried that my sixth-grade year," Amy complained.

"I think the bigger problem," I declared, "is how little time we have to finish getting ready!"

"This is going to be a bigger disaster than last year's fall carnival," Autumn announced.

Now I really did frown. I'd thrown myself into planning the fall carnival. It had been my first big project on SAC, and after seeing how organized I was with some of the smaller events, Ms. Bates had let me take on a lot of responsibility in planning it.

And everything had gone perfectly. That is, until Travis Meyer had to play his stupid prank and ruin the entire event.

The little kids were all loving the hayride, being pulled in a cart by Rob Martin and his horse. But then Travis "freed" the horse. Travis's dog had chased after the horse, and the two of them ended up on a rampage through the pumpkin patch, squashing most of the pumpkins, before making their way over to the ball pit, where the horse crashed into one of the plastic poles holding it up, and all the balls went everywhere. The parents of the two kids who were in the pit were screaming, and the carnival was, suddenly, over.

Of course, it went without saying that we were not allowed to have any kind of animals at any future events.

"We could cancel . . ." Ms. Bates began.

"No!" Autumn, Marc Mancini, and I all said at the same time.

"It's tradition!" Amy added.

"Plus, we ordered everything before winter break," I said. Even though by *we* I actually meant *I*. "If we can get the bouncy house people and at least two food trucks to agree to the new date, we'll be all set."

"Emma, can you take the lead on contacting the outside vendors about the new date?" Ms. Bates asked.

At that moment, I realized that Ms. Bates sounded just like the regular Ms. Bates. Somehow, I'd been expecting her to act, well, weird after going on a date with my father.

"Emma?" Ms. Bates said when I didn't respond.

"Right. I'm on it."

"Great—thank you!" Ms. Bates said, so enthusiastically that Autumn turned to me and raised just one side of her mouth like the smirking emoji as if to ask, *What the heck?*

I tried to ignore Autumn and nodded at Ms. Bates, dutifully writing change date to next Saturday in my to-do notebook.

"I'll be sending out a shared doc with all the other jobs you guys need to sign up for—or find volunteers for," Ms. Bates announced. "That's it, gang. Have a good day."

I hurried to follow Autumn out of the library, pretending to be in a rush so I wouldn't have any excuse to stay behind and talk to Ms. Bates.

It was one thing to hear about how their date went from my dad . . . I did not want to hear about it at school.

Not yet anyway.

Besides, with the carnival now coming up fast, we all had our work cut out for us.

At lunchtime, Theo sat with me and Hallie. I wondered where Frankie was, but I didn't see him anywhere in the cafeteria.

"The carnival date has to change," I declared as I plunked my tray down on the table.

"Seriously?" Hallie asked, looking up from her sandwich.

I nodded as I took the seat beside her. "Apparently it has to be next Saturday. But we still don't have a plan set for the seventh grade's table. You know, last year, the seventh-grade class sponsored a kissing booth. But I guess that's pretty unsanitary."

"Not to mention regressive and problematic," Theo said.

I rolled my eyes. "In English?" Sometimes I wondered if Theo would be a professor someday like both of our dads.

"Well, they promote old-fashioned gender stereotypes, for one," Theo said.

"Okay, I wasn't really going to suggest we have a kissing booth anyway," I argued. "I just felt like a spontaneous vocabulary lesson would be super fun."

Theo balled up his napkin and threw it at me.

"Anyway," I said, "about our carnival table . . . I thought about maybe face painting?"

"I could help with that!" Hallie said excitedly. I knew she loved anything to do with art.

"I'd let you paint my face, Hallie," Frankie said, appearing with his tray.

I smiled at Frankie as he sat down beside Hallie. He always seemed friendlier around Hallie.

Then an idea struck me.

Maybe . . .

Could it be?

Even though Cupid wasn't here (because, of course, no dogs allowed at school) . . . maybe my pug and I were sort of a matchmaking *team*. Maybe I'd just found Hallie the perfect date for the Valentine's Day dance. She'd already told me that she planned to go. And it was obvious that she and Frankie got along well.

I grinned to myself. I'd just found a match for my best friend!

"What kind of designs could you do?" Frankie was asking Hallie.

Hallie smiled as she dug into her mac and cheese. "I do a great sugar skull design, but I guess that's more of a fall look."

"Sounds cool, though," Frankie told her.

I took a bite of my sandwich to hide my smile. Even without Cupid's matchmaking magic—or mine—it seemed like Hallie might be on her way to getting a date for the dance.

"Why are you smiling like that?" Theo asked in my ear.

"I'm not smiling."

"Liar," Theo said. "Whatever it is, I'll figure it out."

"Always so sure of yourself."

"Well, I am a full year older," Theo said with a grin, because he knew how much I hated to be reminded. This time, I threw *my* napkin at him, but he just kept grinning.

* * *

I opened the door to my house and knelt down to greet Cupid. I gave him several kisses and scratched his soft ears. He gave me a bunch of sloppy kisses in return.

"You ready for a walk?" I asked him, and he danced happily in reply.

"Just wait until I tell you what happened at school today," I added as I managed to fit his wriggly body into his halter.

"What happened?" Ms. Bates asked me.

I jumped about a foot in the air, and when I came back down, I saw that there was Ms. Bates standing in our foyer beside my dad, both of them smiling away like this whole thing wasn't weird at all.

6

Just Weird

"Hi, Emma," my father said. "I hope you had a good day at school?"

I nodded, unable to stop staring at Ms. Bates. Seeing her here, in my house, instead of at school, was like my two worlds crashing together.

"Hello, Emma," Ms. Bates said, smiling at me. "Your home is lovely; I was just telling your father. I love these old Highbury houses."

I tried not to frown. I knew that Ms. Bates wasn't in love with anything about Highbury.

"I was just about to give Abby a tour," Dad told me. Then he turned to "Abby" and began to do just that. "As I was saying, the house was originally built in 1859, but my grandfather did quite a bit of renovation, as you can imagine."

Ms. Bates (I could *not* think of her as Abby—too, too weird) followed Dad upstairs as he pointed out the carvings on the wooden banister.

Cupid put a paw on my foot to remind me of what we'd been about to do—well, what he needed to do outside—before we'd been interrupted by our surprise visitor. I pushed open the door, and he sprinted ahead of me toward the grass.

As Cupid sniffed around, I imagined Dad and Ms. Bates having a wedding right out there in our backyard. What would that be like?

I supposed I could order flowers from Lilybelle—daisies would be nice for a summer wedding, and they would suit Ms. Bates. My dress could be a light yellow. Not everyone can pull off yellow, but it looks pretty good on me.

It wouldn't be a sit-down dinner—instead we'd have delicious appetizer-size bites from one of the good restaurants downtown.

And maybe petits fours instead of cake, since Dad wasn't a big fan of sweets anyway . . .

Cupid had finally finished sniffing the entire yard (which means I'd been standing there quite a while) and was sitting at my feet, staring up at me. I realized I'd just planned my dad's entire wedding in my head.

Which was weird too. Did I *want* Dad to get married to Ms. Bates? Or did I just like planning things too much?

"I'm being silly," I told Cupid, scratching behind his ears. "It's just one date. Well, now two, I guess."

I led Cupid back inside, wondering if Dad was still giving the grand tour of our house.

I was hanging up Cupid's halter in the foyer when Dad coughed behind me.

"Emma," he said when I turned around. "Abby's using the bathroom right now, but she and I were planning to head to Francesco's for some dinner. Would you like to come along?"

"Sure . . ." I heard myself saying, before realizing that maybe I should have offered to stay home and eat leftovers so the two of them could have a real date. "I mean, actually, I have a project for history due tomorrow. I need to hop online with my partner, um, Autumn . . . Maybe I could order a pizza so I could work on it?"

"Of course, if you need to work." Dad reached into his pocket and pulled out way too much money for one pizza. "You should invite Autumn over to work with you. We could pick her up before dinner."

"No! I mean, you don't need to do that. I think she has to be home for some kind of . . . family birthday." Man, once I'd started lying it just kept coming. I couldn't remember lying to my dad before.

"Oh. Okay, honey. But definitely order some food. Order whatever you like. We'll just be a couple of hours. Text me if you need me, okay?"

"Okay!" I said, my voice coming out a bit too brightly. Ms. Bates walked into the foyer, and I waved to her and Dad as they put on their coats and headed out the door.

Then I sat down on the last stair, feeling a bit lost. Cupid came and sat right beside me, my faithful little friend. At that moment, I was even more glad than usual to have him. It seemed like it would have been kind of terrible to be alone.

A few minutes later, I heard a soft knock at the door. I got up and peered through the peephole to see Theo standing there wearing a hoodie, his holey old basketball shorts, and the ugly black slippers I always made fun of.

"Hey," he said when I opened the door.

"What's up?" I asked him.

"Well, I was on the porch talking to my dad, and we saw your dad walk by with Ms. Bates. I just thought maybe you could use some company? I mean, I can only guess that this must be . . . weird."

"That's the word all right," I said. "So can you bail on dinner with your parents?" I held up the pile of bills Dad had left. "I have pizza money."

"Done!" Theo said, vaulting over the back of the sofa and grabbing his phone to text his parents.

Even though Cupid was wonderful company, he couldn't have a whole conversation with me. I was glad Theo was here. I smiled and picked up my own phone to place the order. I didn't have to ask what Theo wanted on his pizza. That's the best part about old friends, I thought. Most of the time, you don't even have to ask.

7

Ugh, Travis

"Thank you so much! We'll see you on Saturday."

I hung up the phone at Ms. Bates's desk with a satisfied smile. Freddy's Fries was the last food truck we needed to have a complete carnival experience. I'd also lined up a bounce house for the littles, and a few other places to serve snacks and drinks. Luckily, I knew I could always count on Shana and Stella at Morning Mugs to show up, even at the last minute, with a table full of homemade goodness. It was Highbury magic in action, and I loved it.

Ms. Bates walked back into the library. "My meeting's finally over. So, how did you make out?" she asked me.

"Good. We're all set."

"Great!" Ms. Bates answered with a smile, and I was struck by how pretty she looked. Her hair, which she usually wore back in a boring, low ponytail, was down, and she'd added some waves to it. And she was wearing a little eye makeup, which she never used to do. Not that a person should have to wear makeup, I reflected. But Ms. Bates did look nice.

It seemed like there could only be one reason that she was looking different these days. But I didn't want to think about that too much right now.

"Well, my lunch period's starting, and I'm starving," I told her. "I'll email you all the vendor info."

"Thanks, Emma. You're the best."

"No problem," I told her. I stood up from her desk and headed out of the library.

I stopped off at my locker to pick up my lunch—half a left-over sandwich from The Elephant, stored carefully with a small ice pack. But when I got to the cafeteria and reached our usual table, I nearly lost my appetite.

Ugh. Hallie was sitting with Travis Meyer. And laughing loudly at something he'd just said.

With a frown that I couldn't have wiped off my face for a million dollars, I sat down beside her.

Hallie turned to me, her eyes sparkling. "Oh, hey, Emma— you know Travis, yeah? And Travis, you know Emma?"

Travis was in eighth grade, like Theo. But I certainly knew him. As the carnival ruiner. I nodded at her.

"Everyone knows Emma," Travis said with a smirk. "You're the one who plans everything around here."

"I don't plan *everything*," I said defensively. "But I did plan the fall carnival," I added pointedly, remembering the disaster Travis had brought about.

The smirk disappeared from Travis's face. "Look, Emma, I've been meaning to tell you, for a long time actually . . ."

He paused, and I decided to cut him off. What explanation— or apology—could he possibly give for ruining my event last year? I didn't even want to hear his pathetic attempt at either one.

"Just forget it," I said to Travis.

His face fell. "Okay. Well, I'll get out of here. Hallie, see you later."

As soon as Travis was gone, Hallie turned to me with a glare.

"What'd you have to do that for?" she whispered.

My jaw dropped. "How can you even ask me that? You know what happened at the fall carnival! You were with me and Ms. Bates when that dad at the ball pit screamed at us! And it was all Travis's fault."

"It sounded like he was about to explain . . ."

"How could he possibly explain, Hallie?" I burst out. "What could he say?"

"I don't know, but you didn't even give him the chance."

"What were you talking about with him anyway?" I asked as I unwrapped my sandwich.

"He's my partner in art class this term. We're doing a huge project together. So it would've been really nice if you'd given him a chance." Hallie spoke quietly without meeting my eyes.

"I'm sorry, Hallie. If it were anybody else. But I just . . . can't. Not with Travis."

Hallie balled up the remains of her sandwich and shoved it

into her lunch bag. She didn't say anything else. We sat there in uncomfortable silence until I'd finished eating my sandwich in record time.

After the lunch bell, Hallie walked with me toward our lockers.

"Are you mad at me?" I asked, turning to her as I opened my locker.

"Of course not," Hallie said. But the way she slammed her locker door seemed like maybe she actually was.

The next day, Hallie seemed to be acting more normally around me, and I was glad, but not really surprised. I couldn't imagine Hallie letting someone like Travis Meyer come between us. Not when she and I had been best friends since fourth grade.

I'd been worried for a minute that maybe Travis liked Hallie . . . and what if he asked her to the Valentine's dance? And, worse, what if she actually said yes?

It seemed clear that I'd need to step up my efforts to get Frankie locked in as Hallie's date in time for the dance.

I remembered how Frankie had said that he'd let Hallie

paint his face at the carnival. Maybe the carnival would be a good place to start. What if Frankie was in charge of a booth that was right beside Hallie's face-painting booth?

As I walked into the cafeteria, I saw that Hallie had beaten me to our table again, only this time, luckily, there was no Travis in sight.

"I forgot my lunch, and it's stew day," Hallie said when I sat down. She let a huge blob of stew plop from her fork to the bowl beneath.

"You can have half my sandwich," I said right away, unwrapping my lunch and grabbing the knife from her tray to cut the turkey and avocado with sprouts in half.

"Thanks," Hallie said, her voice brightening as she pushed her lunch tray away.

"So for the face painting," I said, "what else do you need besides the paint you sent me the link for?"

"Nothing," Hallie said around a mouthful of sandwich. "I mean, just brushes and a few jars for the water, but I can get those from the art room." She thought as she chewed. "And maybe I'll make a poster with some sample designs. The last time I painted little kids' faces they had a hard time making a choice. I ended up giving almost everyone a star or a flower."

"Stars and flowers are nice."

"Yeah, but they're not exactly a challenge for my artistic talents." She grinned. "Hey, speaking of which, I finished that pair of earrings I was telling you about. I realized when I was done that they were for you." She unzipped the front pocket of her backpack, pulled out something small, and handed it across the table to me.

"You're so sweet! Thanks, Halls," I said. I unfolded the aluminum foil packet and saw a pair of large earrings, with red crystal beads arranged like two tiny chandeliers. They were cute, but not at all my style. I couldn't ever imagine actually wearing them, but I told her, "They're really pretty!"

"They go perfectly with your dress for the Valentine's Day dance."

My heart sank. *Oh no! I couldn't possibly wear these earrings to the dance.* But somehow I heard myself lying. "Yeah," I said. "They'll be great."

Too bad I'd planned super far ahead—as usual—and found

my dress for the Valentine's Day dance over winter break. Of course I'd shown it to Hallie the very next day.

Thankfully, Frankie appeared then, so I didn't have to keep lying. "Hey," he said, sitting down beside me.

I'd have been happier if he'd sat beside Hallie. "Hey yourself," I said. "So, how's your first full week at HMS going?"

"So far, so good," Frankie said, taking one of my potato chips and popping it into his mouth. "The school lunch here is tragic, though," he said. "Back home in Baltimore we had the best cafeteria. On the last Friday of the month, we had crab cakes."

"We have some good stuff," I said, feeling defensive of the school, even though I almost always packed my lunch. "The peanut butter fudge is amazing."

"Yeah, that is pretty good," Hallie agreed. "But they only make it once a month."

"I'll watch out for it, but in the meantime, I'm having my mom get me some Lunchables or something," Frankie said. The bell rang. "Well, see you guys later," he added, getting up and walking away before I could figure out anything else to say.

I frowned as I tossed out my trash and followed Hallie out of the cafeteria. My plan to get Frankie to ask her to the dance was off to a dismal start.

Maybe, I thought, I *did* need Cupid to actually set things in motion, just like he had with Annie and Frankie's brother. I knew from Annie's online posts that she and Mateo were officially going out. Which was great. They made such a sweet couple.

And, of course, Cupid's magic also seemed to be working with my dad and Ms. Bates, though I was less certain whether that was a good thing.

To get Frankie to ask Hallie to the dance, maybe Cupid had to work his magic on *them*. Which meant I'd need to get Frankie, Hallie, and Cupid together all in the same place.

Then it hit me—the carnival! I could just bring Cupid to the winter carnival, which I'd been planning to do anyway. Sure, animals were technically no longer allowed at any carnivals (thanks to Travis), but Cupid was extra well-behaved, and I'd keep him in his stroller the whole time. Frankie and Hallie would both be there. And then everything would fall perfectly into place.

8

Sandwich Twins

As I was setting up the paint and brushes for the carnival face-painting table, someone came up behind me and put their hands over my eyes.

"Guess who?" a girl's voice asked.

Cupid wasn't barking at all, which meant it was someone I knew. The smell of lilac perfume tipped me off.

"Annie!" I whirled around and stepped into a huge hug from my former babysitter.

Annie is just one of those naturally happy people, but she looked even happier than usual. Her cheeks were pink from the cold, and her dark brown eyes were bright. Her glossy brown hair was pulled back in a perfect messy bun that was somehow surviving the breeze. And then I saw, standing just behind her, Frankie's brother, Mateo—who looked equally happy.

"So . . . how is everything going?" I asked Annie, but Cupid's indignant yelp reminded her that she hadn't said hello to him yet.

Annie went over to Cupid's stroller and he rolled over for her to scratch his belly.

"Oh, Cupid looks so adorable in his winter coat!" Annie cooed. "Is this a new one?"

I nodded. "I just couldn't resist getting it. Doesn't he look good in green?"

"This dog has more coats than I do," Mateo said, but he too reached down and scratched Cupid's belly. "What a cute little guy."

"When does the carnival start?" Annie asked me.

"In twenty minutes." I looked down at my watch. "Oh no, make that fourteen minutes!"

"Well, I'm sure it will be amazing. Your events always are."

"Aw, thank you, Annie. But it's not my event."

"Uh-huh. Sure it's not." Annie winked at me. "Well, we just wanted to say hi. Frankie's around here somewhere," she added, with what seemed like a significant look. What did that mean? Why was she bringing up the fact that Frankie was around?

But then she and Mateo were already walking off, holding hands. I watched them go with a smile—Cupid's first match! Then I shook myself mentally, remembering that I had a lot to do before the opening of the carnival.

I glanced around. The face-painting table was pretty much set up, but where was Hallie? I could handle the prep work, but if I were the one to actually paint the faces, we'd run out of customers very fast. Drawing something on a regular flat surface was difficult enough for me!

I remembered that Hallie had said she'd bring a friend from art class to help her. Maybe she was off meeting that friend.

"Emma!"

I heard Hallie calling my name and turned around. My best friend was walking up to the table. Beside her was none other than Travis Meyer. My heart dropped. *Oh no.* Was *Travis* the art class friend she had mentioned?

I tried not to let a scowl show on my face. I peered behind Travis and was relieved to see that, at least, he didn't have his bounding brown dog with him this time.

As Travis and Hallie stopped at the table, I leaned down and whispered to Cupid, "Why aren't you barking?" Weren't dogs supposed to just *know* when people were no good, and bark at them? But Cupid just gazed back at me, confusion in his big, round eyes.

"Hi, Emma," Travis said. I nodded back at him wordlessly.

"Travis is going to help me with the face painting," Hallie said quickly. "He promised."

"I did," Travis said, shooting Hallie a look I couldn't figure out.

Why was everyone being so strange today?

"Excuse us a second," I told Travis, and pulled Hallie by the arm away from the table.

"Why are you yanking me?" Hallie asked, snatching her arm away.

"You know why! I told you I couldn't forgive Travis . . ."

Hallie raised her chin a notch. "You said to find someone talented to help me. And Travis is the best artist in our class."

My face was burning. "But you remember what happened at the fall carnival . . ."

"I want to give him another chance. And I want you to give him one too."

Hallie sounded serious. I opened my mouth, but I didn't know what to say. She didn't wait for me to answer; she just went back to the table and started moving around the supplies I'd set up.

And then I heard Travis exclaiming, "What a cute dog!" I looked over to see that he was reaching into the stroller and petting Cupid, who had traitorously rolled over to expose his belly again, just as he had for Annie. He accepted Travis's scratching with his tongue lolling out the side of his mouth. "So different from my big mutt."

Yes, I thought. *Much better behaved.*

I walked back over to the table, trying to focus on the face-painting setup. "Okay, well, everything should be ready," I told Hallie, "and I put you near the fountain in case you need to change the water for your brushes." I still felt a little shaken by Hallie's proclamation. It wasn't like her to disagree with me.

My little pup added insult to injury by giving Travis a slobbery kiss. Hallie laughed and leaned over, accepting her own friendly licks.

"It's two tickets per customer," I told them, trying to get everyone back on track. "Unless the customer wants a complicated design—like on their whole face—and then it's four. Just be sure to keep it moving. If the littles can't decide on a design, you may have to basically pick one for them."

Travis gave me a salute, and I frowned harder at him. Then he chuckled. "Emma, I have three younger sisters. I'm good with little kids."

Travis had three little sisters? How did I not know that?

"Okay, well, text me if you need anything or have any problems," I said. "I'll be back by as soon as I've checked on a few things."

"Okay, bye," Hallie said, but she didn't smile. She sat down in the chair Travis had pulled out for her.

I pushed Cupid's stroller away, still shaking my head and muttering under my breath. As I started down the main path, I nearly ran into Theo, who was carrying a giant armful of stuffed fish.

"Hey, Em. You should come see our EA table. It turned out awesome!" He paused when he saw my expression. "What's wrong?"

"Nothing, just a project not working out the way I'd planned." I patted Cupid's head distractedly. "I'll come see your table. I was going to check in on every table anyway."

Theo gave me a smile, like he found me amusing, but I decided to ignore it. I followed him to a green-and-blue table. EA stands for Environmental Activists, one of several do-gooder clubs that Theo is a part of at our school.

They'd strung up a big banner over their booth that said (DON'T) GO FISH!, with the ocean painted underneath.

"Great banner!" I said, admiring it.

"Thanks. I got Hallie to paint it."

"Oh, cool. I didn't know she was doing that." I usually knew everything Hallie was up to. I wondered when she'd had time to paint it. "So, what's the object of the game?" I asked.

"Well, it's a play on that old carnival game where people throw Ping-Pong balls into bowls with real fish in them," Theo explained. "Our fishbowls don't have any fish in them, because that would be inhumane. It's also to symbolize the fact that our oceans are being poisoned," he added solemnly. "If you get two balls into the empty bowl, you win one of these stuffed fish. And everyone gets a pamphlet about ways people can cut down on plastic waste and help our oceans." Theo grinned broadly.

I had to smile at his enthusiasm, and his weirdly creative idea. "Sounds great. The kids will love it," I told him.

I looked around and saw that Mr. Carver had started letting people in the front gate of the park. The carnival had officially begun.

"I've gotta go," I told Theo. "Dad's bringing sandwiches from The Elephant at noon. He's bringing your usual, unless you want something else?"

"No, that'd be great. Thanks, Emma!" Theo's first customers were already stepping up to the table. I waved goodbye to him and headed toward the cotton candy stand, where several members of the cheer squad were working. They seemed to know what they were doing, so I kept moving. I checked on the hockey team, who didn't have anyone there to take tickets, so I drafted Danny Lewis, a kid from my grade, to help out.

Next, it was time to check on Ms. Bates at her book swap table. She didn't have any customers—understandably, not many people remembered to bring a book with them to the carnival to swap, or wanted to carry one around with them as they ate and played games. But Ms. Bates still hosted the book swap table every year.

Just like last year, she sighed and said, "No one reads in this town, Emma! That's the problem."

I promised her that my father would bring her a book (he'd told me this morning) and a tuna salad sandwich from The Elephant—her favorite. Ms. Bates looked more cheerful at that.

I checked on Skee-Ball, the popcorn stand, the dime toss, and the Anime Club's drawing table. Everything was humming along smoothly. Mr. Martin was giving hayrides in his tractor around the back of the park, and, of course, Shana's and Stella's table full of goodies from Morning Mugs was already crowded with customers.

I looked down at Cupid with a satisfied smile. Everything was going very well.

I glanced up and saw Travis walking toward me. Well, maybe not *everything*.

"Hey, Emma!" he said.

I stiffened. "I thought you were working the face-painting booth . . ."

"I am, but Hallie sent me to ask you if you could find someone to help us take tickets and refill our water and everything."

I nodded. "I'll get someone to help you guys, and I'll send them your way."

"Cool. Thanks, Emma," he said, and headed off.

"Travis, wait!" I called. He turned around. "What kind of sandwich would you like? From The Elephant—my dad's bringing lunch."

It was only polite, after all. Even though it was Travis.

"Oh, thanks! They have a turkey sandwich—with avocado and sprouts? I like that one."

"I'm familiar with that one," I told him. He'd just described my usual. "Consider it done."

"That's so nice. See ya!" He gave Cupid another quick pet before scampering off.

Cupid sat up at the edge of his stroller, tail still wagging.

"Okay, so he's polite," I said to my dog. "But don't forget he's not *always* so nice. Especially not at *carnivals*. He may like dogs, but he couldn't keep his safe and under control. No matter how much you enjoy his belly scratches!"

Cupid let out a short bark. Was he actually disagreeing with me? Not him too. I frowned at the possibility.

Just then I spotted Frankie Castillo, wandering around the carnival and checking out the booths. I had an idea.

"Frankie!" I waved him over to me. "How are you enjoying the carnival?"

"It's okay. My brother basically dragged me here."

I decided to ignore his negative comment. "You need to have your face painted—really get in the carnival spirit. Remember how you told Hallie she could paint your face? I think that if everyone sees someone as cool as you with a great design, her table will get a lot more business," I suggested with a bright smile.

Frankie's face turned a little bit pink at my compliment, but he smiled and nodded. "Okay, Emma. I'll get my face painted. If you go with me."

I glanced at my watch. I'd been planning to take another lap around the carnival and check on everyone again, but that could probably wait for a few minutes.

Frankie pointed at the Skee-Ball booth and started walking that way, but I took his arm and began steering him back toward the face-painting table. "I was going to win you something," Frankie said.

"That's so nice, but no time," I said. I kept marching, one arm pushing Cupid's stroller, the other steering Frankie.

"That's right, you pretty much run the events, don't you? Hey, I can push the stroller for you," he said, stepping in front of me and taking over pushing. I couldn't decide if I found it nice or bossy, but focused on getting him over to Hallie.

We reached the face-painting table, and I saw a long line had formed.

"It looks like they're doing okay," Frankie said. "Not hurting for business at all."

"Yes, for now. When I came by before, no one was here," I lied.

Hallie finished painting a little girl's face to look like a yellow butterfly. The girl giggled happily when Hallie showed her a hand mirror, then stood up.

Still steering Frankie, I stepped in front of the next customer, a teenage girl I didn't know. "He was here before and they were out of paint," I explained with an apologetic smile. "He's got a rain check, so he just needs to go next. I'm so sorry." The girl frowned and stepped back. "I'll give you some extra tickets for your trouble," I told her, and handed her some extras I'd stashed in one of the handy side pockets on Cupid's stroller. She shrugged as she accepted the tickets. Luckily she didn't complain or leave the line.

I pushed Frankie into the chair facing Hallie. "Here's your next customer," I told her. "Frankie's really excited to get his face painted."

Hallie looked a little confused about my helping Frankie to butt in line, but she didn't say anything about it. "What kind of design were you thinking of?" she asked Frankie as she swirled her paintbrush in the dirty water. Which—oops—reminded me . . .

"Frankie," I said, "after you get your face painted, could you do us a huge favor and hang out here and help these guys?" I hadn't *forgotten* Travis's request for someone to help. I'd just been *distracted*. "Hallie needs someone to refill her water and keep track of the tickets and stuff. We'll get you lunch, of course, for helping."

"Sure, I can help," Frankie said. "I don't know what kind of design I should get, though. What do you think, Emma?"

"Hmm. Maybe a pirate?"

"I can do a great zombie. It's extra tickets, though," Hallie said, still wiping off her brushes.

"She does do a great zombie," Travis chimed in.

"Okay, zombie it is," Frankie agreed.

"Just don't make it too gross," I pleaded. "Not that Frankie could ever actually look gross. I mean . . ." I blushed. I'd kind of meant that he was too cute to look gross even as a zombie, but I couldn't exactly say that out loud.

Hallie just shrugged. "Okay," she told Frankie. "Close your eyes."

"No prob," Frankie said, smiling at Hallie and doing as she said.

I watched them with satisfaction as Hallie got to work. Everything was off to a great start already! Before I knew it, Frankie would be asking Hallie to the Valentine's dance.

Although . . . I had the nagging feeling that I was forgetting something—but what?

"Emma!" someone yelled from the dunk tank. "There's a problem over here!"

Uh-oh. I couldn't worry about Frankie and Hallie right now—there was a dunk tank crisis to deal with!

"Be right there!" I called back. Before I turned to go, I asked Frankie, "What kind of sandwich would you like from The Elephant?"

He shrugged. "Roast beef, I guess."

I pulled out my phone to text the order update to my dad.

Roast beef. That was Hallie's favorite. They were sandwich twins—that had to be a good sign.

Then, pushing Cupid quickly in his stroller, I zoomed across the carnival to see what was happening at the dunk tank.

When I got home from the carnival, pushing Cupid's stroller up our front walkway, I felt so relieved, just like I always did when a big event ended well. There had been a couple of hiccups— Travis being there, for one, although at least he'd managed not to spook any horses or dogs, and the snafu when the dunk tank had started to leak—but overall, Ms. Bates and I had agreed it was a great success.

It wasn't until I was lifting Cupid out of his stroller that it hit me—the big thing that I'd forgotten! I let out a groan. My whole plan had been to bring Cupid, Hallie, and Frankie together at the carnival so Cupid could do his matchmaking trick. But Cupid had been strapped into his stroller the whole time, so he hadn't been able to leap forward and kiss each of them!

I carried Cupid up to my room, feeling foolish. But, I told myself, it had been pretty hectic all day at the carnival. I'd kept Cupid in his stroller, safe, for a good reason. It wouldn't have been worth it to matchmake Frankie and Hallie if it meant my pup got injured or loose. (*Or* got me in trouble for breaking the no-animals-at-the-carnival rule.)

I sat down at my desk to write in my journal. There would just have to be some other event—before the dance, of course—when I could get Hallie, Frankie, and Cupid all together. And then another idea struck me: a party!

My birthday was in a week. I'd told Dad already that I didn't want a party, but I could tell him I'd changed my mind. The party could be something small and casual, at our house. But it would be a natural way for Frankie and Hallie to come together, since usually everyone was so busy with after-school activities.

I tapped my pen to my lips. The party would need a theme, obviously. Or something to make it special. As I looked down at Cupid, who was still in his cute green jacket, I realized what it could be—a costume party! I already had the perfect costume for Cupid that I hadn't been able to use last Halloween.

I opened my journal and began to make a guest list.

The first step to any successful event was, of course, a good plan.

9

So Much for Plans

"Here you go, Autumn," I said as I handed her one of my birthday party invitations.

They were pretty clever, if I did say so myself. I'd ordered various doll-size outfits online, along with tiny clothes hangers, and each printed invitation was attached using the hanger's hook.

For Autumn's invite, I'd chosen a tiny dress with red sequins. It was one of the fancier ones. I wasn't proud of the feeling, but I did sort of want Autumn to be impressed with my invitations.

"Oh wow, these are really . . . *extra*," Autumn said, but I was pretty sure she was only acting cool. I could tell from her face I'd surprised her, and there was no way she'd be missing my party.

"Fully extra," I agreed. "Wait until you see the party."

As I walked away I realized I'd just promised to top the last school party I'd hosted at my house—which had included a really great nacho bar and a take-home bag of goodies. Now I needed to go even bigger.

But I soon faced a new problem when I sat down beside Hallie at our table in the cafeteria.

"I know what costume I'm gonna wear to your party," she told me excitedly. "I'm going to be a zombie."

I immediately thought of Frankie. Now, I know people should like each other for who they really are, and not what they look like on the outside . . . but I do get the feeling that wearing a bunch of makeup that makes it look like your flesh is decaying is probably not the best way to convince a boy to ask you to a dance.

"No!" I said. The word just burst out of me—I couldn't stop it.

Hallie looked surprised. "What do you mean, *no*?"

I took a breath. "Not, *no*," I sputtered, then took a deep breath before going on. "I just mean, are you sure you don't want to save being a zombie for Halloween? I mean, it's *such* a Halloween look. Besides, I was kind of thinking we could do something together." That was a little white lie, but I was starting to feel desperate to keep Hallie from looking all decayed at my party.

"Em, I can't really afford to shop at the kinds of sites that you—"

"I could get the costumes!" I jumped in.

Hallie made that face she always makes when she's about to be stubborn. "You don't need to buy my costume," she told me.

"I don't mean . . . I mean, I didn't . . ." Suddenly I felt like I'd wandered into the deep end of a swimming pool, and although my feet kept trying to find the bottom, they just couldn't, and I was sinking fast.

Hallie and I didn't ever really talk about money. The thing is, my grandfather was some kind of fancy engineer and made a lot of money, which he left to my dad when he passed away. So I know my dad and I are very lucky since we don't really have to worry about how much stuff costs, but Hallie and her mom do.

I always offered to pay for whatever I could, and sometimes I'd even sneakily cover things. But Hallie gets sort of weird about me paying, sometimes.

I took another deep breath and tried one more time to get out of the deep end. "You're the most creative and artistic person I know. I'm sure you'll come up with an amazing costume idea," I said. "Even if it is something like a zombie, even though zombies *still* give me nightmares," I added, trying to lighten the mood.

Hallie gave me a half smile. "You hate scary movies—you never watch them. How would zombies even get *into* your dreams?"

"Blame Theo," I told her, feeling lighter now that the weight of our almost fight seemed to be lifting. "He's made me watch a ton of that stuff."

"Blame me for what?" Theo asked around a mouthful of apple as he sat down beside me.

"Emma says you got her to watch horror movies," Hallie told him. "When did that happen?"

"Last fall. First, I pretty much dared her that she wouldn't watch *Poltergeist*. And then when she made it through that one by holding her hand in front of her face for more than half of it, I challenged her to watch a few more."

"I can't believe it," Hallie said, shaking her head. "You always say no to me when I try to get you to watch anything scary! You wouldn't even let me rent *Coraline*."

"I'm kind of with Emma on that one. Those black button eyes are way creepier than ghosts or zombies," Theo said with a shudder.

I beamed at Theo for taking my side. "Oh, I almost forgot!" I reached into my small shopping bag of invites and found Theo's. For him, I'd chosen a tiny astronaut suit complete with a miniature space helmet.

"Wow, Emma—you've really outdone yourself this time!" Theo said. "And this space suit's so cool—I think George definitely needs to wear it."

"That's what I was thinking," I said, feeling happy that Theo appreciated my creative invites.

"Who's George?" Hallie asked.

"It's just this stuffed rabbit that I've had forever," Theo said.

"He sits on top of my computer in my room. Sort of like a good-luck charm."

"Theo used to have to have George with him *all* the time," I added with a grin.

Theo rolled his eyes. "Are you sure you want to start trading embarrassing stories from when we were really little? Because I'm older. I remember more. Like this one doll that got lost—"

I put up a hand. "No! I yield. I'm sorry." I turned to Hallie. "Theo is all grown-up now and terrifically mature, and George is just a . . . souvenir of his youth."

Theo had been taking a swig of milk, but he snorted some of it out as I finished my statement. "A *souvenir of my youth*? Emma, sometimes you really do say the craziest stuff."

I smiled even though Theo was teasing me. I was still just so glad that I'd managed to defuse whatever had happened between Hallie and me.

The rest of the week seemed to drag. Who could stand to listen in class when there was an event to plan? Almost everyone had told me that they were coming to my party on Saturday, and after school each day, I checked off at least one item on my planning to-do list.

When Saturday afternoon finally arrived, I got a bunch of stuff set up in the kitchen. Then I checked the time. Hallie was supposed to come over and get ready, but she hadn't shown up yet, so I went upstairs and put on my costume. I was going as Hermione Granger from Harry Potter, partly because I secretly wished that my school had an old-fashioned uniform like the ones they had at Hogwarts. I'd ordered it online and was happy with how well-made the skirt and sweater were. I was relieved it all fit, because I had to match Cupid.

I pulled on the knee-high socks and smiled at how cute they looked. For just a moment, I wished that there were a boy coming to this party that *I* wanted to impress. But then I decided I was just being silly, and got out the costume I'd been dying to put on Cupid since the fall: He was going as my sidekick, Harry Potter.

I'd gotten his costume online too—specially made, even. I'd had to send in his measurements. I'd planned ahead with plenty of time before Halloween, but then my order had gotten delayed!

We'd had to put together a backup costume at the last minute, which I wasn't happy about. But today was the perfect opportunity to show off what had eventually come in the mail. At least the waiting had paid off. The tiny wizard cape, glasses, and tie fit him perfectly. The costume even included a little stick-on lightning bolt scar, but I figured I'd try affixing that right before everyone got here.

Cupid didn't look entirely pleased at being dressed up, but I kept feeding him small bites of his favorite treat. He let out a few small sighs but didn't fuss as I tied on the tiny gold-and-red-striped tie.

"Oh my gosh, Cupid!" I cried. I gave him a hug—carefully, so as not to muss his cape, and stepped back to see the full effect. Then I scooped him up and held him beside me in front of my full-length mirror. "Adorable!"

"Yes, you are the fairest of them all," said a low voice behind me, and I nearly dropped Cupid as I jumped.

"Sorry," Theo chuckled, standing in my doorway. "I just couldn't resist since I caught you admiring yourself."

"I was admiring *Cupid's* costume," I told him, and rolled my eyes toward the ceiling.

"Well, yours is pretty cute too. I just came early to see if you needed any help setting up."

"I really do!" I said, relieved. "Hallie was supposed to come early, but . . . anyway, never mind. I need to finish getting all the snacks set up downstairs."

"Aren't you going to comment on my costume?" Theo asked.

He did look pretty good in his Doctor Strange costume. "We're both wizards, how funny."

"Excuse me, I prefer master of the mystic arts."

"Oh, lord. Come on, *master*, let's get the snacks ready. You too, tiny Harry Potter." I called Cupid away from the nap he'd already started taking, with his cape flowing out around him on the floor.

Cupid and I followed Theo down the stairs. I realized as my stocking feet slid a bit on the wooden floor that I'd forgotten my shoes and would have to go back up to get them.

"So how come you changed your mind about having a

birthday party?" Theo asked. "It seems like just the other day you were announcing that you didn't need a big thing this year."

I shrugged. "I just changed my mind, is all. I've been trying to figure out how to have a costume party before Halloween anyway."

"Great costumes!" Dad said as we reached the bottom of the stairs.

"You don't know who we are, do you, Dad?"

Dad stroked his chin and glanced down at Cupid. "Well, I believe that Cupid is that character Harris Potter. I know that much." Then he looked up at me with a triumphant smile. "So, you're probably Harris's . . . sister, am I right?"

Theo laughed. "Harris Potter! Mr. W, you crack me up."

"Was I right?" Dad pressed.

I giggled. "Close, Dad, very close. Can you help us put out the snacks?"

"Of course," Dad said as we all headed into the kitchen. "But who is Theo?"

Theo smiled. "It'd be more of a pop culture deep cut for you, sir."

"He's a wizard," I said drily.

"Oh, okay. Very nice wizard costume."

Now Theo rolled his eyes, and I threw him a huge bag of pretzels to open.

"Oh no, I forgot to make the punch!" I slapped a hand to my forehead in dismay, ignoring Theo's chuckle at my dramatics. "I don't know how I'll get everything done before people start getting here."

"I take it Emma overplanned again?" Theo asked Dad.

"I don't *over*plan . . ." I started to protest but then realized Theo was probably right. "Okay, I give up. I guess that's fair. I'm just glad you're both here to help." I walked over to the refrigerator and opened the door. "Dad, would you mind making the punch? All the ingredients are here together in this part of the fridge. And, Theo, can you preheat the oven to three-fifty? I have a few hot appetizers."

"Hot appetizers for a middle school party. Yeah, you don't overplan." Theo smirked, but he did start pressing buttons on the oven.

"I just admitted that I did!" I said, and my voice came out

higher than I'd intended. "Sorry, Theo. I'm just nervous, I guess. I've never thrown a costume party before."

Theo put one hand on each of my shoulders. "Hey. It's going to be great, Emma. Everything you plan is great."

The way he was looking at me, so serious, made me feel even more nervous. Suddenly my Hermione cardigan felt much too heavy, and I smiled at him before stepping back and then shrugging out of my sweater. "Thanks. I don't know why I'm so nervous."

"I don't either," Theo said. He frowned for a second and then turned back to the stove. "Where's the preheat button again?"

"Wow, you do *not* take after your mom."

"Yeah, I guess I'm more of a book guy, like Dad," Theo agreed, sounding like his usual cheerful self. The frown had disappeared. "Although we're both intrepid travelers . . . and Dad's practically Indiana Jones."

I rolled my eyes. "Yeah. Practically."

"Okay, punch is ready!" Dad announced from where he stood by the counter, stirring a big bowl of yummy-looking punch. I was impressed. "What's next?"

"Cupcakes!" I declared. "They need to be taken out and put on a plate."

Dad frowned. "This is so much junk food, Emma. Are you sure you don't want me to chop up some vegetables to put out?"

I gave him a look. "You can chop them if you'd like, Dad. But I can pretty much guarantee no one's going to eat them. Especially since Stella from Morning Mugs made these cupcakes."

With a sigh, Dad seemed to give up on his vegetable dream.

I pulled appetizers from the freezer, and Theo helped me prep them all on baking sheets. Well, he opened bags and I did the rest.

"I'll get the egg rolls and pigs in a blanket in the oven, Em," he said. "I'm older, so I should handle the appliances."

I made a face. "I barely trust you with the scissors."

Dad pulled the sheets from my hands. "I'll do it. Are you both ready?"

Theo side-eyed me. "Emma, you can finish putting on your costume. People will be here soon."

"I'm ready, though," I protested.

"Shoes? And you took off your sweater and left it somewhere."

"Oh, I guess you're right. You stay with Theo, Cupid."

I ran upstairs to put on my shoes and noticed my cell phone sitting on the bed. I saw I'd missed a couple of text messages from Hallie.

SO sorry Em but I am super sick have the WORST cold. So. Much. Snot.

Can't come 2 the party 2nite.

Plz take lots of pics 4 me!!!

My stomach dropped. What?? How could Hallie be sick? I'd just seen her yesterday and she'd been perfectly fine. I'd only planned this *entire* party to bring her together with Frankie so that Cupid could do his magic. This was a disaster of epic proportions.

I heard music coming from downstairs and realized Theo must have jumped in and picked something to play.

"Emma! Guests are starting to arrive!" Dad called from downstairs.

With a frown, I grabbed my phone and headed downstairs. A couple of girls from my grade had come early.

I put on a big, fake smile, and welcomed them to my (now useless) party.

What's wrong? Theo mouthed at me from across the room.

I walked over to him. "Hallie's not coming. She's sick."

"Emma, I know she's your best friend, but the party will still be fun."

"You don't understand. I . . ." I stopped myself before admitting that the party was mostly a matchmaking scheme.

His eyes narrowed; he was suspicious of my almost comment. But then I distracted him by asking, "Did you make a playlist for the party?"

He smiled. "I did. You'll love it."

"Thanks." I nudged his shoulder with mine. "What would I do without you?"

"Lucky for you you'll never find out. Hey, man!" I turned to see that Frankie Castillo had just arrived. Theo stepped forward and held out a fist for Frankie to bump.

"Hey," Frankie said to Theo. Then he smiled at me. "Cute costume, Emma."

He was dressed as a zombie—just like Hallie had wanted to—in tattered clothes. His makeup looked really good. Had Hallie somehow done Frankie's makeup? But she was sick . . .

"I love your makeup," I said. "Who did it?"

"I heard you were a fan of zombies," Frankie said. Beside him, Theo snorted. Frankie gave him a confused look before continuing. "Anyway, Hallie was gonna do it, but when she texted and said she was sick, I got that kid Travis to do it. He's really good."

Just then Travis walked in the door, dressed as Han Solo from Star Wars. It was actually a pretty great costume.

I looked at Travis in confusion. I hadn't invited him—so Frankie must have. Why was Frankie inviting people to my party, though? Sure, Theo could invite whoever he wanted, but that was different. The privilege definitely did not extend to Frankie. But Frankie just smiled at me and gave Travis a fist bump, and then Theo joined in admiring the zombie makeup job.

"Come on, Cupid," I called, and turned to walk away. When I realized my buddy wasn't following me, I looked back to find him sprawled on the floor getting another belly rub from Travis. I groaned. Why Travis? Besides, Cupid sprawling in that undignified way was going to wrinkle his costume!

I decided to try to ignore Travis, and forget about the fact that Hallie was home sick, missing the perfect opportunity to bond with Frankie. I went into the kitchen and helped myself to some of the punch. It was the fancy kind with a lime sherbet mold of a flower in the center, and it really was delicious. Then I realized that since I hadn't eaten dinner, some of the hot appetizers would be a good idea. I made myself a little plate and then wandered back out to survey the party. It was a good turnout, and a few people were even dancing, which would make DJ Theo happy.

When I looked over at him, he was indeed grinning at me and waved. A girl from his grade walked up to him and asked him to dance, and he shrugged and went with her to the center of the room, where Dad and I had cleared out the furniture for dancing.

Autumn made her usual late entrance, wearing a completely over-the-top costume: Marie Antoinette. She wore a gigantic, ruffle-covered pink gown and a wig of huge blond ringlets tied with matching pink ribbon. The other girls in our grade oohed and aahed over her costume, but I had to fight to keep from rolling my eyes. I should have known that Autumn would try to find a way to turn my party into some kind of competition.

She walked over to me. "Great party, Emma," she said. "Sorry it took me so long. This outfit is very hard to get into!"

"I can see why," I said. "It's very impressive."

"Thanks!" she said, and whirled away in a flurry of ruffles.

"Autumn's got to Autumn, I guess," said Theo, who was dancing nearby, and I had to laugh then.

The rest of the evening passed in a pleasant blur of snacks, costumes, congratulations on the excellent party, and even a bit of dancing for me. I found that I could do a funny sort of slide move on the slick wood floor once I took my shoes off again. Frankie came and danced near me, grinning and pointing to his zombie makeup, but I hadn't quite forgiven him yet for inviting Travis. Though I had to admit, Travis was kind of the life of the party. He kept pulling people off of couches to make them dance, and everyone seemed to love his costume.

Before long, Dad came out from his study and pointed at the clock, and since almost everyone saw him do it, the party began to break up. Everyone started texting their parents to come get them.

As people began to trickle out, Theo and Dad helped me clean up. For some reason, Frankie was still there too. Cupid stood watch at our feet, on the lookout for one of us to drop some snack crumbs. Finally, Dad offered to take Theo home so he didn't have to walk in the dark, dressed as a wizard.

"I can take you too, Frankie," Dad offered.

"My brother's actually on his way. Thanks, though."

Dad looked at the clock again. "Are you sure? It's getting pretty late."

"Yeah, totally—Mateo's coming; he just always gets sidetracked."

Theo gave me a look like, *Is this okay?* I shrugged. I figured if Mateo was coming, then Frankie could hang until then. I had a dog to walk, and then I couldn't wait to get out of my costume and read a little before going to sleep. I hated to admit it, even to myself, but I maybe liked *planning* parties a little bit more than actually *being* at parties.

Theo followed Dad out the door, and when I turned back toward Frankie, he was grinning.

"Finally!" he declared.

"Wait, what?"

"I thought they'd never leave. But I'm so glad to finally get a chance to ask you . . . I mean, I'm sure you know *what* I'm going to ask . . ."

A feeling of unease was prickling its way up my spine. I took a step back away from him. "No, I definitely don't know."

"Oh, Emma, you don't have to play it that way. I know you like me." He took a step closer. "And I definitely like you."

I stood up straight. Did kids really just *announce* to each other who they liked? Based on what I'd learned at sleepovers and from people like Autumn, crushes were usually passed around via whispers and "Guess what I heard?" But here was Frankie flat-out telling me he *liked* me! He couldn't like *me*!

"Frankie, I think you're confused," I started. "You like *Hallie*."

"Hallie?" Frankie's eyebrows shot up. "I mean, she's really cool, but I don't . . . What would make you think that?"

I threw up my hands in frustration. "Oh, I don't know, because you've been hanging around her for the past two weeks?" I suggested. "And you had her do your makeup at the carnival. And I saw that you posted the picture of your makeup on your profile? You even tagged her!"

"*You* dragged me over there and cut me into the line to get my face painted," Frankie pointed out. "And the pic was the one *you* took—I tagged you too, remember?"

Oh, right. He had.

"And, since apparently you haven't noticed," Frankie went on, his face flushing a little, "it's *you* I've been hanging around."

"Oh . . ." I put my arms around my middle, suddenly feeling a little bit sick. All those tiny hot dogs had formed a ball of badness in my stomach. My brain was replaying every interaction I'd had with Hallie and with Frankie since he got here. What had I done?

"But I thought you liked *Hallie*," I said again. My voice sounded much smaller and less certain now.

Frankie crossed his arms over his chest too. "I don't know

why you're so stuck on that. If you just gave me a chance . . ." Frankie's voice had gotten kind of loud.

"I think it's time you were leaving, young man."

Frankie jumped. My father had used his best professor voice and was standing in the foyer, watching us.

"My ride's here anyway," Frankie said, and stomped out the front door without another word.

Dad gave me a questioning look, but I just shook my head and ran past him, up the stairs to my room, slipping a little on the way in my stupid stockinged feet.

I heard the front door open and close. Dad was taking Cupid out for me.

When Dad brought Cupid upstairs a while later, I'd gotten myself mostly together. I sat on my bed, still in my Hermione costume. Cupid sat on my rug, looking up at me with worried eyes. He could always tell when I was upset.

"Are you okay, Emma?" Dad asked.

"Yeah. Sorry. I was just . . . It turns out I'm very stupid."

"I won't hear talk like that," Dad said. But he didn't use his professor voice; he said it gently. He sat down on the chair closest to my bed. "Just because that boy was being foolish, I don't want you blaming yourself."

"But I should have *seen* it. I didn't know that he . . . didn't know he liked me." My cheeks felt warm. I didn't usually tell my dad about stuff like this. But then, I guess I'd never really had anything to tell.

"And did you tell him that?" Dad asked.

I sniffed back a few tears that were threatening to break through. "Yeah."

"Then you didn't do anything wrong. Emma, I know that you're very grown-up for your age in many ways, and that you are often able to . . . direct people. But that does not mean that you will always know just what people are thinking, or what they are going to do. You still have a lot of growing up to do, after all."

"Now you sound like Theo," I told him, trying to smile.

"Well, Theo is a very sensible boy. And if he were here, I'm sure he'd remind you that he *is* a full year older than you."

I smiled for real then. "I'm sure he would. Thanks for taking Cupid out, Dad," I said, and picked up my little fur ball for a much-needed doggy hug.

"Of course. It really was a very nice party, you know."

"Up until the end."

"Don't let one misunderstanding ruin your night," Dad said with a squeeze of my shoulder. "I hope you had a nice birthday?"

"I did. Thanks, Dad."

"Happy birthday, sweetheart. Good night."

"Night, Dad."

Just as Dad was closing the door, my phone buzzed and I gave a start. The text was from Theo.

Are you okay? Did Frankie leave?

Yeah. But . . . he sort of asked me . . . I THOUGHT he liked Hallie . . .

Uh oh. I was kind of afraid you thought that.

Did you know that he—that Frankie—liked me?

Three little dots danced for an uncomfortably long time before Theo's answer came through.

I guessed, but I didn't know. Are you ok though???

I'm ok. Just feel stupid.

You're not. I'm sorry, Em.

It's ok. Thanks for helping tonight.

It was a real nice party. Night, Em. And happy birthday. C u tomorrow 😔

Night, T.

I turned off the light and pulled Cupid closer, listening to the rapid beat of his heart in the dark and wishing my own would slow down so I could get to sleep.

As of today, I was a whole year older. But I felt more foolish today than on any day of the year that came before.

10

Bugs Are a Snack, Not an Entrée

Of course, Monday started with me running into the exact person I'd been hoping to avoid. I spotted Frankie on my way to the library and immediately dropped all the sign-making supplies I'd been carrying.

He knelt to help me gather up the markers that had rolled in all directions.

"So," he started. I sucked in a breath. "If you're so surprised to see me, does that mean you've been thinking about what I asked?"

"What do you mean, what you asked?"

"Well," he said, stretching out the word as he handed me the pile of poster board. "I didn't completely get to finish asking . . . about the Valentine's Day dance . . ."

My stomach in knots, I tried half-heartedly, "But Hallie . . ."

Frankie stood. "I already told you, Emma. Just think about it, okay?" He hitched his backpack higher on his shoulders, turned, and headed off down the hallway.

How was Frankie not as mortified as I was by this whole thing? He'd even tried to ask me *again* about the dance, while I'd been planning on avoiding him all week. But it seemed like he was saying that he hadn't given up just yet, no matter what I said to him about Hallie.

At lunch, Frankie was sitting there at our table as though nothing weird had happened between us. Then I found out that we had something in common: the same birthday week. As soon as Theo came to join us, he said, "Happy birthday, man."

I felt my face whip toward Frankie's in surprise. "What? It's your birthday? Today?"

"Yep. We're almost birthday twins," he added with a wink. *A wink!* "So, my parents are getting to be friends with Theo's parents, from soccer. And my mom invited them to come to dinner tonight. You should come too."

I realized a few seconds later that Frankie had been talking to me, since he and Theo were staring at me.

"Oh! I mean . . . I guess so. I could go." Frankie seemed to be pretending things were normal . . . I could do the same, right? And Theo would be there. Anyway, my previous plan for tonight had been yet another pizza night, since Dad had another dinner date with Ms. Bates. I looked over at Hallie. She was texting somebody and paying absolutely no attention to Frankie or to me.

I guess I really had been off the mark there, on both sides.

"Great!" Frankie said. "It's a restaurant downtown—I think it's called The Hungry Hippo?"

I had to laugh at that. "The Ravenous Ram." Since it was one of the three really nice places to eat dinner in Highbury, it wasn't hard to guess.

Frankie flashed another wide smile at me, and it was like for the first time I was actually looking at him . . . at his sparkling brown eyes, and thick, wavy dark hair . . .

"Your dad can come too," Frankie was telling me.

"Oh, thanks . . . but he has a date."

"Okay." He shrugged. "Theo, let's go over to the soccer table. You have to see this video Jason showed me . . ."

The two of them left with only a quick apologetic smile from Theo. Hallie was still texting, so I pulled out my own phone and sent her our favorite emoji, the one that looks like Tinker Bell.

Her head shot up. "Hey," she said, like I'd just gotten there.

"Who are you texting so much?" I asked.

"Oh . . . it's just for a class project. So, Frankie asked you to dinner?"

"Well, and his parents, and Theo and *his* parents."

"Guess that's not a date, then." Hallie shrugged, tucking her phone into her pocket.

"Nope," I said, still feeling weird about everything I'd been secretly planning for Hallie and Frankie. Thank goodness I hadn't told her. "Are you feeling better?"

Hallie nodded. "My throat still hurts, but Mom said since I didn't have a fever anymore I needed to go to school. I'm really sorry again that I had to miss your birthday party."

"Me too! But please don't apologize—you didn't ask to get sick!"

"No, but I'm still sorry I missed it. You have to tell me everything that happened," she said, finally perking up. "I was still recovering yesterday—Mom made me stay in bed and wouldn't even give me my phone."

"I will," I agreed. "Maybe we can go to Morning Mugs after school tomorrow?"

"I've got a thing . . . with my project. But later this week. For sure."

The bell rang, and we walked together back to our lockers. Just as I was putting my phone away before class, it dinged. Hallie had sent me back Tinker Bell and three yellow hearts.

When I got home from school, I gave Cupid a huge hug and let him kiss my face.

"Oh, Emma—the germs!" Dad exclaimed as he met me in the foyer.

"I read online that people's phones have more germs on them than dogs' mouths."

"Ugh," he complained, "I don't know if I want to know that. Anyway, you should be careful believing what you read online." He had that stern look in his eye, but he also petted Cupid's head as he trotted by.

"Are you still having dinner with Ms. Bates tonight?" I asked.

Dad nodded. "But I don't want to leave you home alone eating pizza again. You should come with us."

"I can't. I was invited to Frankie Castillo's birthday dinner. Is it all right if I go?"

Dad's eyebrows narrowed together to form a single V. "That new boy from your party? I don't know, Emma . . ."

"It was just a misunderstanding," I rushed to say. Why had I told Dad any of it? "He's nice. And besides, his parents, and Theo, and the Knights will be there. We're going to The Ravenous Ram."

"Oh," Dad said. He seemed to be studying me, but went along. "Well, then, that's fine, of course. The Ravenous Ram?" I could tell by his face that he'd been planning to take Ms. Bates there too.

"It's okay if . . ." I began.

"Abby and I are going to drive over to Lititz," he apparently decided in the moment. "There's a new place we've been meaning to try."

I gave him a doubtful look, but he sounded resolved, so I didn't push it. If they'd been meaning to try this new place, tonight was a great night, I figured. The Ravenous Ram was small, and I didn't want to watch my dad be on a date, or have him watch my potentially awkward dinner with Frankie. I'd have to join my dad and Ms. Bates eventually, but at least it didn't have to be tonight.

After I fed Cupid and took him for a short walk, I brought him upstairs with me. I waded into my closet to find the right outfit, but it proved harder than usual. Nothing seemed right. Everything I put on felt like I was trying too hard, and then when I changed into a pair of dark jeans and a plain white T-shirt, that looked too casual. It wasn't as though most people at The Ravenous Ram would be all that dressed up, but still.

I heard Theo talking to Dad downstairs, and looked over at Cupid in alarm. I definitely did not want to be caught having an outfit meltdown by Theo of all people. He always teased me when I took a long time to get ready. I gathered up all my discarded choices in a huge ball and shoved them into my closet. As I was about to cram the door closed, I spotted a scarf that had belonged to my mother hanging on a hook. I grabbed it, along with my nice black wool jacket. I was slipping my feet into black ballerina flats when Theo came in, unannounced as usual.

"Wow, you look really nice," he said.

I shot him a wary look. "You sound surprised."

"No, I just meant . . . you look sort of . . . grown-up in that outfit."

I wrinkled my nose. "In a good way or a bad way?"

Theo laughed. "A good way." His eyes narrowed a bit. "Hey, you're not nervous about how you look in front of *Frank*, are you?"

I bristled. "I think he just goes by Frankie, and no, of course not."

"Frankie sounds like a dog's name. No offense, Cupid." Theo leaned down and gave Cupid some head scratches. Cupid rolled over onto his back, so then Theo had to crouch down and give him some real attention.

Was I imagining that Theo sounded sort of snarky about Frankie all of a sudden?

"I'm kind of surprised you said yes to this dinner," Theo went on, keeping his attention on Cupid. "I thought you felt weird about the whole Frankie-Hallie thing?"

I fiddled with my scarf. "Well, he didn't *exactly* say no to her. I mean, he didn't even know I was trying to get them to go to the dance together."

"That's what all of this has been about?" Theo asked. "A date for Hallie for the dance?"

"Well, you know, these things require planning," I said. "Otherwise a girl might end up with no one to dance with."

Theo glanced up. "Is that what . . . girls . . . want?"

"I don't know!" I shrugged. "I'm not trying to say what every girl wants." I pushed past him and started downstairs. "Girls want all kinds of things. Come on, Cupid."

"Well, sure, of course," Theo mumbled as he followed me downstairs.

Dad was pacing in the foyer, no doubt ready to leave to pick up Ms. Bates, but waiting for me. "Emma, you should take a scarf," he told me.

"I'm wearing a scarf."

Dad's eyes refocused on my outfit. "I meant a winter scarf. But," he said with a small smile, "you do look lovely in your mother's scarf. She'd be so pleased you're wearing it."

His eyes brightened, and his voice quavered a bit.

I felt Theo squeeze my hand once. Then he let go and called down as he ran back upstairs, "I'll get a winter scarf for her, sir."

"He's a good kid," Dad said, and I realized he meant Theo, who was already clomping back downstairs holding a fluffy pink scarf.

"He definitely is," I agreed while Theo was still out of earshot.

By the time the Knights and I reached The Ravenous Ram, the Castillos were already seated at a big table in the back room. I saw that Mateo had brought someone—Annie! We both called each other's name in delight.

"I see it's going well," I said in Annie's ear as she hugged me.

"Yes!" she said. "Thanks to Cupid!"

There was a fireplace in the back of the room, already burning with a cheerful fire, and the table was set with wineglasses for the grown-ups. I smiled. I loved going out for a nice dinner—not just for the food, but the whole atmosphere. Maybe someday I'd host dinner parties of my own. The one and only drawback to a fancy restaurant, as far as I was concerned, is that they're almost never dog-friendly. I felt a pang of missing Cupid, even though I knew he was safe at home playing with his favorite squeaky toy.

As I sat down, I looked across the table at Frankie, who looked very handsome in a white shirt and jacket. He grinned at me, and I felt my face turn pink. I pulled at my winter scarf, suddenly feeling way too hot to wear it a second longer, but managed to make it tighter somehow, and I made a strangled sound.

Theo chuckled beside me, then reached over to untangle the scarf.

"Thank you," I said in a low voice. My face was even redder, I was sure, now that my best friend had needed to save me from my own scarf.

I felt the silk scarf at my throat and realized the careful tie job I'd done in my room was now all messed up. But without my mom's scarf, I would feel underdressed, since Mrs. Knight, Mrs. Castillo, and Annie were all wearing skirts or dresses. Even Theo was wearing the nice charcoal-colored sweater I'd gotten him for Christmas, with a white button-down shirt underneath.

I excused myself to go to the restroom, even though we'd just arrived at the restaurant. Ignoring Theo's questioning glance, I hurried off to the bathroom. Inside, facing the mirror, I pulled the twisted, and now wrinkled, scarf from my neck. I stared at my reflection for a few seconds, frowning. "Get it together, Emma."

"Are you okay?" Annie had walked into the restroom just in time to see me fighting with yet another scarf.

"Yeah. I just . . . everything I'm wearing is wrong, and now I can't figure out how to retie this stupid scarf."

Annie came closer, took the two ends of the scarf from my hands, and started adjusting it. "I don't think this scarf is stupid. I think you look stylish in it." She stepped back as she finished tying. "There, now you're all put together again."

I nodded. "Thanks, Annie." I followed her back to the table and we sat down.

I picked up the menu and began to read, although I pretty much knew everything on the Ram's menu by heart by now. I always ordered the same thing: the wood-fire-grilled chicken, which was so tasty and also had the benefit of being Dad-approved, since there was nothing about it that he considered unhealthy. Although, I considered, tonight seemed like the perfect night to swap the steamed vegetables for mashed potatoes, since Dad wasn't here to judge.

"Ooh, bacon-wrapped scallops!" Frankie exclaimed, eyeing his menu. "What do you say, Emma?"

Frankie was seated across from me, and he turned his wide smile on me.

"Emma doesn't eat bacon," Theo said from behind his menu.

"No bacon! That's outrageous." Frankie leaned forward. "You just don't know what you're missing."

"I *have* eaten bacon," I told him. "But my dad is very serious about processed meats being bad for you, so I try to avoid it. But I'm sure one small bite of an appetizer would be okay."

"Besides, your dad's not here." Then Frankie actually *winked* at me again as though he were some hero in a movie or something.

I couldn't believe he didn't feel awkward about how I'd reacted to him at my party.

Still from behind his menu, Theo turned to me and rolled his eyes.

I frowned at him and turned back to Frankie. "Do you know what you're getting? Everything here is super good."

"Have you tried everything on the menu?" Frankie asked in surprise. "I mean, I guess you must have since there aren't really any other restaurants in town."

I thought I saw Mrs. Castillo frown at Frankie's comment, and I felt the urge to defend Highbury.

"Actually, there are, and no, I haven't really tried *everything*, I've just been here with people who have. I always get the same thing."

"I would have guessed you were a more adventurous eater," Frankie replied.

I put my menu down. Why did it feel like Frankie was criticizing me?

"What do you always get, Emma?" Mr. Knight asked. It felt like he was trying to rescue me. "Maybe I'll have that!"

"The chicken," I said. "I just know what I like. I'll try any food once. Well, *almost* anything. I wouldn't eat bugs, like Theo."

Frankie looked at Theo, who was laughing. "Just as a snack, not an entrée," Theo said.

"Insects and worms are a common snack in Thailand. We all tried them, but Theo actually *liked* the roasted crickets," Mrs. Knight said.

"He liked them so much he ordered a bunch online after they got back and tried to get me to eat them!" I exclaimed. "But I draw the line at eating any sort of insect."

"Yuck, that's disgusting," Frankie agreed. "I'm with you, Emma."

"Have you ever tried any?" Theo asked. He was sitting up in his seat and sort of staring down Frankie. But Frankie just laughed.

"No, man, just the thought of it is too gross for me."

Just then our server arrived and everyone began ordering. I felt for a moment that I really should try something different, but I was the third to order, and I couldn't pick something else fast enough, so I ordered my favorite chicken dish after all.

Theo ordered probably the most interesting dish on the menu, a fish called branzino. Frankie ordered the fanciest, the lobster with steak.

When the appetizer came, Frankie took two of the juicy bacon-wrapped scallops and put them on his plate before passing the platter across to me. "Try one, Emma?"

"Don't tell Dad," I said to Theo, and popped one into my mouth. It was rich and savory and delicious.

The rest of the meal passed by quickly as we all focused on eating. I ate every bite of my favorite meal, glad I hadn't let Frankie sway me into changing my order.

All through dinner, Frankie asked me about Cupid and the school events I'd planned. Annie partly talked to the adults, but then would listen in on us too. She caught my eye and shook her head with a smile. I shrugged back at her.

At the end of the night, I said goodbye to Annie, Mateo, Frankie, and Frankie's parents. Then I headed off with Theo and his parents since they were giving me a ride home. The Castillos were still waiting for the valet to bring their car as Mr. Knight pulled away. They waved to us as we drove past, and I thought I saw Frankie give me another one of his winks.

When I got home, after plopping down on the floor to snuggle with Cupid—and then taking him for a short walk—I carried him upstairs. I stepped out of my shoes and carefully untied my mom's scarf. Annie had done such a good job tying it—I hoped I'd be able to do it again the same way. It had made me feel closer to my mom, somehow, wearing something of hers.

I sat down and opened up my journal. Lately I'd been thinking of my mom pretty often, but somehow whenever I tried to make sense of my thoughts about her and get them down on paper, I just froze.

After staring at the blank page for a few minutes, I found myself writing about Frankie.

> I was afraid that Frankie would never talk to me again after my party.

I stared at the words for a few seconds and then wrote another sentence:

> But now I'm starting to worry that... maybe... he still likes me.

The next logical sentence to write would be about how *I*

felt about Frankie Castillo. But I realized I couldn't answer that question, so I closed my journal.

So much for getting in some writing before bed. I realized one thing for sure. When less had been happening in my life, I'd been writing so much more!

11

Surprise!

Now that the carnival was over, it was time to get cracking on plans for the Valentine's Day dance. I headed to the library after school and found Ms. Bates wrestling with a very large picture book of Scotland. She had the protective cover either half on or half off—I couldn't tell which—and was straining to get it the rest of the way.

"Oh, hello, Emma." She looked down at the book with a fierce scowl and then hurled it down onto the top of her messy desk. I took a deep breath and tried to ignore the urge to tidy things up for her.

"Hi, Ms. Bates. I was hoping we could lay out some of the early plans for the dance. If you're not too busy?"

"No, it's been a quiet day, so I was trying to catch up on some things. But my heart's not in any of it, I confess."

"What's the matter?"

She handed me a book from the top of her desk. It was a new hardcover without a catalog sticker or a clear library cover on it. "What's this?" I asked.

Ms. Bates flopped back into her chair. "Only the future I wanted," she said, closing her eyes. "That book right there was just published. It was written by my college roommate, Laurel."

"Oh," I said, sitting down in the chair across from her desk. "I see." I knew Ms. Bates had always wanted to write a book. She mentioned it often.

"We used to be writing partners—we would critique each other's work. Now she's done it! And what have I done?" Ms. Bates put her head in her hands. "I'm here in Nowheresville trying to protect a book of Scottish castles that no one's checked out since 1998!"

At her words, I felt a bit stung. I was protective of my

town, and wondered if what she said had anything to do with my dad too. Things seemed to be going well between them—they were having dinner a few times a week, and Dad always came back smiling. But Dad loved Highbury. He was a part of "Nowheresville."

But maybe this wasn't about my dad, or Highbury, or anything except how her old friend's success was making her feel. I picked up her roommate's book and quickly skimmed the back cover.

"Ms. Bates, this is a very nice book and all, but it doesn't really seem like your style. I mean, the main character is apparently a werewolf. I'm sure that when you finally write your great novel, it will be even better than this. Not a werewolf in sight."

Ms. Bates looked up at me and laughed. "Oh, Emma—thank you! I'm being silly, comparing myself to my friend. Everyone has their own path. And werewolves can be fun. I just need to get *started*. I do have an idea for a novel that I think might actually go somewhere."

"That's the spirit!" I told her. "I'd love to write a whole book someday."

"Oh my goodness . . . that reminds me!" Ms. Bates cried, her eyes widening. "I can't believe I forgot!"

"Forgot what?" I asked as Ms. Bates began rummaging through the mess on her desk.

"I opened the package with Laurel's book and got sidetracked, but I have some very exciting news!" She searched around her desk until she found a large white envelope, which she then handed to me.

The return address said SOCIETY OF LETTERS, which was apparently in New York City. The envelope was addressed to MS. EMMA WINTERS C/O MS. ABBY BATES, at the school's address. I looked up at her, confused.

"It's for you," Ms. Bates said excitedly. "Open it!"

I took out the letter, unfolded it, and began to read.

Dear Emma Winters,

Congratulations! Your submission titled "Puppy Love" has been accepted as a finalist in this year's Society of Letters Young Writers' Contest. You and your sponsor, as well as one guest, are cordially invited to attend the awards ceremony on January 25, in New York City. The runner-up and winner will be announced, and prizes awarded at that time . . .

"But I didn't enter any contest . . ." I looked up at Ms. Bates, more confused than ever. "I don't even know what this submission is. I didn't write anything called that . . ."

"Yes, you did," she said. "Well, I added the title—it was required to have one to enter. It's the essay you wrote for English last spring—the one Ms. Wilder had you read at that assembly?"

Oh! Of course I knew the one she meant. I'd written an essay about Cupid, and how having a dog made my life with Dad feel a little more complete. It had only been slightly mortifying to read it in front of absolutely everyone.

"Okay . . . but how did these Letters people get it?" I asked.

"I sent it to them," Ms. Bates explained. "I'm a member, and when I saw the Young Writers' Contest in their magazine, I knew I should enter your essay."

I glanced down at the letter again, my heart racing. "I can't believe I won. Well, that I'm a finalist." I looked up at Ms. Bates in wonder. "So . . . when did you send in my essay?"

Ms. Bates seemed to understand what I was trying to ask without asking—whether she'd entered my writing in the contest before or after she and my dad had started seeing each other. "Over the winter break," Ms. Bates replied. "The deadline was January 1."

That was a relief—it meant she'd thought to submit me just as Regular-Student Emma, not Daughter of Her Maybe Boyfriend.

"I can't believe you thought of me," I said, still processing everything, "and that you thought my writing might be good enough to enter."

Ms. Bates beamed. "Clearly I was right! Your piece was selected out of thousands of entries."

Impulsively, I jumped up and threw my arms around her. "Thank you, Ms. Bates!" I said. "For believing in me."

"Of course! I always have," she added. "Hey, I'm supposed to meet your dad in a little while. What do you say we go tell him the news together?"

*   *   *

Ms. Bates gave me a ride home in her tiny yellow car, and on the short trip she told me about some great new books she'd just ordered for the library. I wrote down the titles of the two that sounded the most interesting in my list notebook.

When we told him the news, Dad gave me a big hug. Then he smiled at Ms. Bates and thanked her for doing something so nice for me.

"I'm so excited for you, Emma," Dad said. "You'll have to be careful in the city—it's not like Highbury there. But you'll be with Abby, and she knows her way around New York City. It'll be nice . . . for the two of you to spend some time together."

Ms. Bates nodded. "I'm your sponsor, but it says in the letter you can also invite a guest of your choosing," she told me.

I knew who I should ask. "Dad?"

Dad shook his head, looking regretful. "I have a seminar that evening with my advanced students that I can't reschedule. Looks like you'll need to decide who else you want to ask to go with you." He didn't have to say that I had a tough choice to make between Hallie and Theo.

"Ask to go where?" Theo said as he walked in our kitchen door.

I laughed. Fate—or Theo's crack timing—had just decided for me.

"Do you want to go to New York this Saturday?" I asked him.

Theo's eyes lit up. "Heck yeah!"

I laughed at his enthusiasm. I was excited too, but also a little nervous. I'd only been to New York City once before, for a school field trip.

"Don't worry. It'll be awesome," Theo said beside me, too quietly for Ms. Bates or Dad to hear. I smiled up at him. Clearly he'd noticed the hesitation on my face. And suddenly I felt very sure that he was right.

Cupid pawed at my legs as though he were telling me that *he* wanted to go to New York too, and we all laughed.

Hallie squealed with joy when I told her the news about the contest the next day. She didn't seem sad that I'd asked Theo to come along to New York City. In fact, I thought maybe she seemed just the tiniest bit relieved, since she said that she was really busy right now with her big art project.

At lunch, when Frankie sat down with Theo, Hallie, and me, I told him all about the contest too.

But he didn't have much of a reaction, just shrugged with a half-hearted smile. "You and Theo both getting out of here and visiting a real city. That's great."

Ugh, now Frankie was hating on Highbury again?

He stood up. "I actually have to go get a book for history. Wanna come?" he asked me.

"Hallie is still eating," I said, gesturing to her. I didn't want to abandon her.

"Okay, cool. Later, then."

I frowned as he stalked off.

"I wonder why he's annoyed about your going to New York," Hallie mused.

"Yeah," I murmured. "What's up with that?"

Hallie turned to look at me carefully.

"Do you like him?" she asked bluntly. Theo didn't look up, but I could tell he was listening hard.

"I don't *think* so?" I answered truthfully, and Hallie laughed.

"He just really seems to like you," she said.

"Well . . ." I chewed my lip. "He did sort of tell me that after my birthday party."

"What? Told you he *liked* you?" Hallie exclaimed so loudly that people from the next table turned to look. "How am I just hearing about this now?"

"I don't know . . . I guess I was just sort of . . . embarrassed, or something."

Theo kept his mouth shut about how he already knew.

"Why would a boy liking you be embarrassing?" Hallie rolled her eyes. "Besides, I'm your best friend—you can tell me anything. What did you tell him at the party?"

I shrugged, shifting uncomfortably in my seat. "I guess I pretty much gave him the idea that I didn't like him back." Of course, I couldn't tell Hallie why I'd reacted *so* negatively to Frankie.

"But now you're not so sure?" Hallie asked.

"Well, I *was* sure . . . At first I thought I'd offended him and that he'd never speak to me again. But I don't know if he really heard me. He's just been acting like everything is normal. Well, until now. It just got . . . confusing."

Suddenly Travis Meyer appeared at our table and plunked himself down.

"Hey, Hallie. You're feeling better, right?"

Wait, what? Travis knew that Hallie had been sick? But then I remembered—Frankie had gone to *Travis* to get his zombie makeup done because of Hallie's cold.

"So, was I right about *Gravity Falls*?" Travis was asking Hallie. "Did it help get your mind off your cold?"

Hallie nodded enthusiastically. "It totally did. You were so right."

Wait wait, what what? Travis knew Hallie was sick *and* gave her recommendations on what to watch while she was sick? I'd assumed from her text—and from her missing my party—that she'd been basically sleeping the whole time. But she'd been texting with Travis. And watching some show he recommended.

"You okay, Emma?" Travis asked.

I blinked. "Oh, yeah, I'm fine."

"Oh, 'cause Hallie and I were just saying that we were going to go get a jump on our art project, but you didn't say anything." I looked up and realized that Travis was holding Hallie's tray like he was going to take it over to the trash for her.

"Sorry! I was just thinking about . . . my trip."

"Emma won a trip to New York for her writing," Hallie told him brightly, and Travis put the tray down to give me a high five.

"Way to go, Emma!"

"Thank you," I said, surprised at his enthusiasm.

"I won a poetry award last year, but I only got to go to Harrisburg," he told me.

Travis won an award for writing poetry? Why did I feel like my whole world was making less and less sense every day?

Theo stood up too. "I have yet another makeup quiz to take. You okay if I head out?"

I nodded. "Of course."

Before I knew it I was left sitting alone at the table as the bell rang.

"Oh, Emma, I didn't see you sitting there all by yourself—that's so sad! Next time come sit with us," Autumn told me in a loud voice as she walked past.

I folded my arms and scowled at her retreating figure. Going away this weekend suddenly seemed like the best idea in the entire world.

12

Magic

On Saturday, Theo, Ms. Bates, and I rode the Amtrak train to New York City. In Penn Station, we wove through a crush of people to transfer to the subway, which was a much bumpier and more crowded ride than the Amtrak had been. Ms. Bates explained that the Society of Letters was in a neighborhood called SoHo. Theo said that "SoHo" stood for "South of Houston Street."

When we reached SoHo, I was excited to get out onto the street. We emerged onto Broadway, a loud, bustling avenue. We were surrounded on all sides by office buildings, restaurants, cafés, and sleek clothing stores. Other tourists and serious-looking New Yorkers streamed around us. I stood close to Ms. Bates, feeling kind of overwhelmed. Theo, world traveler that he was, looked thrilled, and was snapping pictures of everything with his phone.

Ms. Bates led us to the tall, old-fashioned building that housed the Society of Letters.

"Here it is!" she announced. "This is a very historical building. Isn't the detailing around the windows beautiful?"

"What time period is it from?" Theo asked her.

"Probably the late eighteen hundreds," Ms. Bates began. My interest wandered from her lesson on the history of buildings to a little dog walking with his owner on a leash. The pup looked up at me as he passed, and I felt a pang, missing my Cupid.

"We're still a bit early for the reception," Ms. Bates was saying. "Do you want to stop and have a cup of tea? Or you kids love your hot chocolate . . ."

"Sounds good to me," Theo said, and I nodded. Hot cocoa sounded great.

When I pointed at a big chain coffee shop across the street,

Ms. Bates said, "We can do better than that!" She led the way to a smaller independent café called It's Bean a While. When we stepped inside, I was surprised that the place reminded me a bit of Morning Mugs back home. I was glad we'd picked someplace owned by people like Shana and Stella, rather than some giant corporation.

"So, how are you enjoying your first trip to the Big Apple?" Ms. Bates asked me as we waited in line.

"I've been here before," I told her.

"Getting off the school bus and walking up the stairs to the art museum for a field trip doesn't count," Theo pointed out.

"Well, I was *here*, is all I'm saying." I stuck my tongue out at him and he shoved my shoulder playfully with his own.

"You kids behave! I promised both your parents that I'd watch out for you."

"Both my parents and Emma's dad know this is how we are," Theo said.

I nodded in agreement. "My dad knows how difficult Theo is to deal with."

"Hey!" Theo said.

Ms. Bates rolled her eyes. "What do each of you want? My treat."

"Oh, no, Ms. Bates," Theo protested, reaching for his wallet. "I can get . . ."

"No, no, Theo, please. It's so fun to show you two around the city. I haven't been in so long."

"Well," Theo said, scanning the menu. "In that case, I'll take a café au lait and a cranberry muffin."

"You drink coffee now?" I gaped at him.

"Sometimes," Theo said, sounding defensive.

"Hot cocoa for me," I told Ms. Bates. "Thank you."

"She's too young for coffee!" Theo told Ms. Bates, and pulled me away to claim one of the tiny tables in a corner.

I hit his arm. "So are you! Does your mom know you're drinking coffee?"

Theo gave me a smug look. "Emma, this is my mom we're talking about. She let me try fermented horse milk in Mongolia."

I'm sure my face reflected my horror. "You drank that?"

"Just a taste."

"Was it awful?"

"Yes, it was," he said, and I laughed.

Soon enough, Ms. Bates joined us with our orders. "Here you go," she said. "One café au lait, and a cranberry muffin. And, Emma, here's your cocoa."

"Thank you," we chorused.

"What were you two talking about?" Ms. Bates asked, settling onto the little stool. "Emma's prospects for winning? I don't know anything about the competition, of course, but your essay is so good, Emma!"

"Thanks, Ms. Bates. And thanks for entering me in the contest. And coming with us."

"Emma . . ." she started as she stirred her tea. "I wonder if, if you might not mind calling me Abby? And you too, Theo, of course. When we're not at school, I mean."

I took a drink of cocoa too fast and burned my tongue a little. I swallowed, then nodded and managed to say "Abby" even though it sounded super weird.

"I'll try, Abby," Theo said with a smile, raising his coffee up for a second as though toasting her. Somehow it sounded much more natural when he said her name.

Suddenly I felt very hot in the small café, and I realized I had to take off my coat, even though I'd planned on waiting until we reached the reception. I stood up and shrugged out of my coat. I was wearing a blue skirt and a nice pink cardigan. Underneath the sweater was a T-shirt I'd ordered online to wear to school next month, on Valentine's Day. I was wearing it today as a sort of good-luck charm.

The light pink shirt was screen-printed with the image of my adorable Cupid, dressed up as his namesake, wearing a pair of wings with a tiny quiver of arrows slung over his shoulder.

"Oh my goodness, what an adorable shirt!" Ms. Bates exclaimed.

"I just thought . . . for luck," I said, and felt my cheeks turn pink to match my sweater and the Cupid shirt.

"It's awesome," Theo said. "Now it's like Cupid's here too."

I smiled gratefully at him for knowing when to *stop* teasing me about my dog-attachment issues.

After a few minutes of enjoying our drinks—which we agreed were good, but *not* as good as those at Morning Mugs—Ms.

Bates looked at her watch and exclaimed that it was time to head over for the reception.

It was just a short walk back, and before I knew it, we were standing in the lobby of the building for the Society of Letters. The Society was on the eleventh floor, according to the uniformed man at the desk. Ms. Bates even had to take out her driver's license so he could make a copy of it. I thought of how often cars and buildings were left unlocked back home and was struck by how different everything was here.

We got off the elevator, and a cheerful teenage girl with very curly hair, who was holding a stack of three clipboards, greeted us right away. "Hi, I'm Britt! Are you all here for the Young Writers' reception?"

I was surprised at the Southern twang of her accent, but then I supposed people from everywhere lived here in New York. "We are," Ms. Bates said. "This is Emma Winters: She's one of the finalists."

"Oh, congratulations to you, Emma. And this must be your sponsor, and your guest." She looked down at her first clipboard, wrinkled her nose, then moved on to the second. Her "organizational system" reminded me of Ms. Bates's.

"Abby Bates and Theo Knight?" Britt asked at last, and Ms. Bates and Theo nodded.

I shrugged out of my coat, and my phone clattered to the floor. "Oh, shoot," I exclaimed, checking it anxiously for cracks. All clear. I remembered why I hated this coat. "Ugh, I forgot, everything falls out of the pockets of this coat when I take it off." I frowned down at my pocket-less skirt.

"Here, I'll hold on to it," Theo said, and I handed him my phone.

"Oh, I almost forgot," Britt said, handing me a fat envelope. "Here's the official application for the Society of Letters Young Writers' Summer Program. As a finalist, you are invited to apply. It's two weeks in the summer, and the courses are taught by published authors. It's very exciting!"

I accepted the envelope from her with a polite smile, but I couldn't imagine spending two whole weeks in the summer here. The city was so big, and so different from Highbury.

"Right this way," Britt told us with a smile, and we followed her into a large room with rows of chairs set up, and a small stage with a podium at the front. On both sides of the room were two tables set with coffee urns, a bowl of punch, and little pastries.

"Cool, second breakfast," Theo announced, before tearing into a mini cheese Danish.

"You all can sit anywhere you'd like," Britt explained. "The presentation will begin in a few minutes. Oh, and congratulations again!"

I looked at Ms. Bates, who beamed at me. She seemed to think I was going to win this writing contest. I looked around the room at the other finalists and their guests. Maybe she was right . . . maybe I could win. After all, no one else could possibly have written about anything more wonderful than my Cupid. I looked down at the program Britt had handed me and skimmed through the titles of the pieces. Some were pretty standard: "My Best Friend" and "The Best Summer Ever." A few titles were very strange, like "WHYBDL," "that tragic duck," and "#nobody." I wondered if the Society of Letters wouldn't prefer someone who knew how to capitalize properly.

"Ladies and gentlemen, please take your seats for the presentation!" a woman at the front of the room called, and Theo came back over to join us. He, Ms. Bates, and I claimed three empty seats. "Welcome to the thirty-fifth annual Young Writers' prize sponsored by the New York Society of Letters. Young Writers, we are so proud of all of you, and remember, you are all winners."

She introduced an author, an older woman with short gray hair; I didn't recognize her name, but Ms. Bates hummed beside me in excitement. I tried to pay attention to her speech, but all I could think about was my essay, and all the other writers in the room. What if an essay about a pug was silly? Ms. Bates had given me confidence, but now doubts chewed at my stomach.

At first it felt like the introduction would never end, but then I still didn't feel ready to hear the results.

"Now, for the announcement of the pieces earning the top prizes this year," the author said, reading off a sheet of paper. "Third runner-up, taking home a one-hundred-dollar gift certificate to Harrison's Books in Brooklyn . . . Paige O'Malley."

The crowd applauded as Paige O'Malley, a tall girl about my age, moved forward and read a paragraph from her story.

She was the author of "WHYBDL," which turned out to be an acronym that stood for several different things in the story. The presenter said her story was "clever and moving," and everyone clapped when she was done.

I felt my stomach tighten into a knot at the suspense as the presenter began to announce the second-prize winner. Theo gave me a grin and raised his hand to show two crossed fingers. I figured I didn't need the top prize, but it would be nice to go home and say that I'd won something, right? But as the presenter awarded the second and first runner-up prizes to other kids, I began to feel more nervous. What if I'd won the top prize after all? Ms. Bates sent me another hopeful smile. My stomach felt queasy and I was glad I hadn't eaten any of the tiny Danishes.

"And finally, this year's top prize . . . goes to Remy Worrell, with his story '#nobody.'"

Everyone began cheering. I felt all the hope I'd stored up in the last few minutes rush out of me, but my stomach was still tight, and I felt my cheeks turn pink. I didn't want Ms. Bates or Theo to know that I'd wanted to win, or maybe even, in a little tiny part of myself, *expected* to win.

Remy Worrell started reading from his story, and suddenly my essay about Cupid seemed very boring and uncreative. Now I felt even more foolish for thinking I might have had a chance.

"I'm sorry, Emma," Theo said in a low voice when Remy finished reading.

"It's okay," I said. The presenter was saying that all the finalists should feel free to continue to mingle. "Can we go?" I asked Ms. Bates. My voice sounded small, and I felt a little pathetic, but at that moment, I just wanted to get out of there. I knew it wasn't very gracious, and I was glad that Dad wasn't there to remind me of that.

But Ms. Bates just nodded once and began to lead the way out. I got a little tangled trying to quickly shrug into my coat, but Theo helped me, and before I knew it we were back outside on the busy city street. The cold air felt good after the stuffy room.

"Well, there were certainly some very avant-garde pieces in the mix," Ms. Bates said. "Who would have guessed that the winner would be the one with a hashtag for a title?"

I had to laugh a little then, because I'd never heard Ms. Bates use the word *hashtag* before. "So, since we have some time before we need to eat lunch, and then get the train, perhaps you'll indulge me in a trip to the Strand?" Ms. Bates asked. "It's that big bookstore I've told you about."

"Sure, Ms. . . . Abby," I told her, still feeling a little unsteady after the unexpected stress of the awards.

We followed her as she began purposely marching toward the subway entrance. "Are you okay?" Theo asked me.

"Sure, why wouldn't I be?" I said as we made our way down the subway steps.

"You just seemed disappointed. Which is totally normal! I know I would be. But, Emma, it was a nationwide contest—it's still a big deal to be one of the finalists who got picked."

"Of course. I didn't expect to win." I hoped my red cheeks didn't give me away.

"Okay." We reached the bottom of the stairs, and I swiped the card the way Ms. Bates had shown me that morning. I went through the turnstile and stepped onto the platform.

"Oh my God—Abby? Is that you?" A woman in a bright blue coat standing on the platform turned and gaped at Ms. Bates.

"Stephanie? What are the chances?" Ms. Bates and the woman were hugging and squealing and jumping up and down. Finally, Ms. Bates turned back to us. "Emma, Theo, this is my dear friend from college, Stephanie Lewis. Steph, these are two young people from my town—I'm chaperoning them; Emma was a finalist in a contest with the Society of Letters."

"Oh, how exciting, congratulations!" Stephanie said to me.

"Thank you. I can't believe you just found each other like that," I said.

Ms. Bates grinned at her friend and then back at me. At that moment, she looked so much younger than she usually did to me. "It's New York City magic," Ms. Bates announced with a wink at Theo and me.

She turned back to her friend, and the two began talking a mile a minute. When the train came, they sat down together, and Theo and I ended up standing, holding on to a pole not too far from them.

"Crazy how she found her friend like that in a city of eight million people," Theo said.

"Yeah, crazy," I echoed. I would not have expected something like that to happen in a place like New York City.

The subway lurched to a stop, and two seats opened up.

As Theo and I sat down, I was thinking that maybe I could practice my writing more . . . maybe find a workshop or two . . . and then maybe I could even enter the contest again next year.

"So, Emma, what do you think about that summer program that they gave you the application for?" Theo asked me. I looked over at him in surprise—it was like he'd been reading my mind.

"Maybe . . ." I began.

"Kids, this is our stop," Ms. Bates called.

The doors whooshed open, and I followed Theo, Ms. Bates, and Ms. Bates's friend out among the crush of people.

"Stephanie and I would love to catch up some more, if you two don't mind," Ms. Bates said to me and Theo once we reached the street. We were standing right by a wide square full of trees and benches and people crisscrossing busily. "We'll all stay in this little area, but you can pick what you'd like to do for about an hour, before we head back toward the train."

I felt apprehensive, but Theo nodded. "Sure! Emma and I can have lunch."

"Are you sure you wouldn't mind, Emma?" Ms. Bates asked.

"Of course not," I said. Ms. Bates showed us the spot near the subway entrance where we would meet, double-checked that we knew where we were about six times, and then she and her friend walked off toward the bookstore, chattering away.

"Where do you want to go?" Theo asked me. "Are you hungry?"

I shook my head.

"Me neither," Theo said. "After eating so much breakfast." Theo paused and looked around. "Well, Forbidden Planet's near here—I'd like to check it out if it's okay with you?"

I nodded, forcing a small smile even though I didn't know what Forbidden Planet was.

In truth, I still felt sort of overwhelmed and out of my element. At that moment, what I really wanted was to be back at home in safe, familiar Highbury.

I followed along behind Theo amid the busy crowd, keeping an eye on his red scarf and charcoal-colored coat. It seemed that everyone in the city was packed in here on these few streets, darting across the crosswalks, carrying packages, each looking very intent on some secret goal of their own.

I looked down and saw an adorable pug walking jauntily on a bright pink leash, and smiled into her dark brown eyes. Her tongue lolled out of the side of her mouth in a way that reminded me of Cupid and I felt another stab of homesickness.

When I looked up, Theo had gotten a little ahead of me, so I quickened my pace to catch up with him. I fell into step beside him again, but when I looked over at him, I almost yelped in surprise.

The person I'd just caught up to was wearing a red scarf and a charcoal-colored coat, but he wasn't Theo. He was much older than my best friend.

I stopped in my tracks and looked around in panic for Theo. I didn't see him anywhere. People streamed around either side of me.

Don't panic, Emma. You know where he was going—just look up the address. Forbidden Planet, he'd said. That was easy enough to remember.

I reached into the pocket of my coat for my phone. And a

fresh wave of panic washed over me as I remembered handing Theo my phone back at the Society of Letters.

I hadn't gotten it back.

I had stopped moving, but people kept swirling around me. What should I do? I didn't know my way around this place at all. Ms. Bates had pointed out the two streets we were meeting on, but I couldn't remember how many turns Theo and I had taken.

My heart was racing, but I told myself to stay calm. I could figure out what to do. I needed to take stock. I'd mostly been following along with Theo and Ms. Bates, but I did remember that the stop we'd gotten off at had been called Union Square. I peered carefully up and down the street and could see the square that we'd started at in one direction. I would just go back. It was a big square, but I could walk to each corner and look around for a place called Forbidden Planet. Or I could see if I recognized which corner we were supposed to meet back at, and wait for Theo to find me.

I decided to split the difference and make one pass around each edge of the square, then take up a spot and look out for Theo.

I began looking at faces as they passed, searching for my friend. I saw people who were very young and very old, with every hair and skin and eye color, and all sorts of different types of clothing. I even saw one teenage girl wearing shorts in spite of the cold! I saw big and small dogs out walking with their owners, people eating food on sticks or sandwiches, drinking coffee or juice. There were vendors in one section of the park, selling vegetables and jewelry and cheese. And this was just one small corner of the city! Every face I saw, I realized, had a story to tell, just like all the kids at the Society this morning.

I'd never really thought of what it would be like to live someplace other than Highbury, but being here had me wondering what life would be like in a big, exciting place like New York City.

A young man wearing a striped coat stepped out in front of me. "Hey there! Sale at the Planet. Have a great day!" He grinned as he handed me a bright green flyer.

I looked down at the flyer in my hand as an amazed smile spread across my face. At the top of the flyer were the words *Forbidden Planet*. At the bottom was printed the address: 832 Broadway.

"New York City magic," I repeated, remembering what Ms. Bates had said. I looked up at the nearest building to orient myself. I was already standing on Broadway. I wasn't sure which direction to go in at first—but there were only two choices!

In just a few minutes, I reached the big comic book store called Forbidden Planet and spotted Theo pacing outside. I felt a rush of relief as I raced toward him, and he crashed into me with a huge hug.

"Emma, you found me! Thank God. I had your phone!" Theo said.

I stepped back and gave him a look. "I know," I said drily.

"I wasn't sure what to do, but I figured since I'd told you where I was going I should stay here. Did you ask somebody how to get here?"

I started to feel a blush creep in as I realized that in my panic I hadn't even thought of that simple solution. I shoved the flyer in my coat pocket and nodded. "Yep. Sure did."

Maybe I'd just keep this particular bit of New York City magic to myself.

Theo hugged me again. "I'm so glad you found somebody

who knew where it was. Come on, let's go find Ms. Bates and get out of here."

"I'm not in a rush," I told him, looking around the crowded streets with new eyes.

Before, I'd just seen a crowded mess—a place that was the opposite of Highbury. But now, for the first time, I saw a bit of magic in a place that *wasn't* my hometown.

13

Surprise 😠

By lunchtime on Tuesday, life seemed to be back to normal. The day I'd spent in New York City felt almost like a dream, though it was fun talking about it with people at school.

Hallie and I were sitting down at our usual table in the cafeteria when Frankie appeared. He looked tired and rumpled and threw himself down onto the bench beside me with a groan.

"Hard night, dude?" Hallie asked.

"Late-night travel is the absolute worst. And I *planned* to sleep for the rest of the day, but my parents said I had to come in."

"Where did you go?" I asked.

"My family went back to Baltimore this weekend. It was my grandpa's birthday."

"Oh, you didn't tell us," I said. "We were wondering where you were yesterday."

"Well, there was all that *excitement* about your New York trip . . ."

He didn't ask how it was, so I said, "Right. Well, did you have fun?"

"I guess. I forgot how much I like it there, actually," Frankie replied. "Anyway, so now I'm here, so as not to miss my all-important classes. What have I missed around here while I was gone? Nothing, I'm sure."

"Autumn Hawkins is running for Queen of Hearts," Hallie told Frankie. "Yesterday she gave out cupcakes with her face on them, so you missed that."

Frankie frowned. "Queen of Hearts?"

"It's this thing for the Valentine's Day dance," I said.

"Seriously? How tacky. The cupcake-face thing, I mean. Do you mean it was like one of those photo cakes?"

"Yep," Hallie said. "Except the picture came out kind of stretched . . ."

Frankie gave a rather evil-looking smile. "Please tell me you have photographic evidence of this huge face cupcake?"

Hallie was nodding and pulling up the picture she'd taken on her phone.

Frankie let out a bark of laughter at the picture and showed it to me, as though I hadn't already seen them live the day before.

"I mean, we already knew she had a big head," I said, and Frankie laughed harder.

But as soon as the words left my mouth I felt a little queasy. Then I looked up and saw Theo was about to sit down beside me, and he gave me a look confirming that he felt the same about us being mean about Autumn. I knew he wasn't her biggest fan, but he never liked talking about people behind their backs.

"Were the cupcakes at least good?" Frankie asked as he recovered from laughing.

"They were pretty dry," Theo admitted.

"Meanwhile, why is our Emma not running for this Heart

Queen thing?" Frankie said. "Surely if there's a queen here in this place, it should be Emma."

I flushed. What did he mean by that? I was most embarrassed that Theo was sitting here to hear it. "That's not really my thing. I'm so busy planning the dance itself," I told Frankie.

"Or Hallie." Frankie grinned. "She's the other prettiest girl at this school. Why are you two letting Autumn steal the crown?"

Hallie rolled her eyes, but she looked a little pleased at being included in the compliment. I felt a rush of hope. If Frankie thought Hallie was pretty, did that mean there was still a chance he would take her to the dance?

"The queen doesn't actually *do* anything," Theo pointed out. "She sits in a decorated chair and gets her picture taken, and that's about it."

"Well, and then she and her partner dance the first dance," I reminded him.

Frankie had stopped listening, and he laid his head down on the table with a loud groan. "I wish this day were over."

"Just three more periods, man," Theo told him, taking a swig from his thermos. I watched his eyes travel to Frankie's

Aquafina water bottle, and I saw him deciding whether or not to remind Frankie about the danger of plastics to our planet. I myself hadn't used a single-use plastic bottle for as long as I could remember. It wasn't worth the wrath of Theo.

"I'll see you guys later," Theo said, clearly having decided to wait to try to convert Frankie into a planet saver.

"Cheer up," I told Frankie. "Aren't you excited for the big soccer game Friday?"

He groaned louder. "Ugh, I forgot about that. That means I definitely have to go to practice after school."

"I'm sure you could skip, after you got in so late last night. Especially if it's going to make you so grumpy," I told him, feeling annoyed at his relentless glass-is-half-emptiness.

"No, I'd feel even grumpier if I let the team down."

I stood up then, and Hallie did too. "These are problems you'll have to solve for yourself. Choose your own level of grumpiness," I told him, and spun on my heel and left.

"I like that—'choose your own level of grumpiness,'" Hallie said as we left the cafeteria. "He really is being a grouch today."

"Yeah," I said. "But I guess maybe he's homesick." Normally

I would feel very sympathetic to a bout of homesickness, of course. But after my adventure in the city, maybe I wasn't as sympathetic as usual.

"Maybe he is," Hallie said. "But, dude, look at *that*."

Autumn had gone next level with her Queen of Hearts run. There, just outside the cafeteria, was a life-size cardboard cutout of Autumn, wearing a sparkly bright pink dress, with a big speech bubble saying *Vote for Autumn!*

"Is she serious?" Hallie asked me.

"Perfectly serious," Autumn said behind us, and we both jumped.

"It's just a little . . . extra," Hallie said. Her face was pink after being caught by Autumn.

"You're entitled to your opinion," she said loftily, then marched away.

I turned to Hallie. "I think she's finally lost it."

"I think you may be right."

The next day, Autumn revved up her queen campaign even further by bribing everyone with a snow-cone machine at lunch. I decided not to eat one, on principle, but Hallie and I were pretty much the only ones who didn't join in.

After lunch, I went to the library for my study hall. Ms. Bates came over to me right after I walked in. "Emma, I just wanted to tell you, if you want to take a step back on the Valentine's dance planning, we'd all understand. I know it's one of your favorite events, but with you in the running for queen, you may not have as much time."

"I'm not—wait, what did you say?" I trailed her back toward her desk.

"Oh, your friend dropped off a flyer and asked me to post it just a few minutes ago. It's such a lovely picture of you!"

She handed me the flyer and I recognized my online profile picture and, below it, the words VOTE FOR EMMA—OUR TRUE QUEEN!

"Who brought this?" I asked Ms. Bates.

"That new boy. Frankie?"

Frankie? Why would *Frankie* do this?

"I didn't know about any of this," I said to Ms. Bates, feeling my anger mount. "It wasn't my idea. I'm not running for queen.

And of course I will still be planning—helping to plan—the dance."

"Okay," Ms. Bates said. She sounded about as confused as I felt.

I couldn't find Frankie to confront him until the end of the day. But before I found him, I saw the poster-size version of the flyer Ms. Bates had shown me, hanging up in the school lobby for all to see. I stopped in my tracks for a solid minute, staring at my own face, before I could march over to his locker and wait for him to appear.

"What's this?" I demanded, thrusting the flyer Ms. Bates had handed me under his nose.

"I told you yesterday you needed to run," Frankie said with a shrug. He slammed his locker shut and began walking away.

I blinked once in surprise at his lack of reaction, then chased behind him. Finally, I put a hand on his arm to get him to stop. I took a deep breath before saying, "You did. And *I* told you that it wasn't my sort of thing. But then you go behind my back and sign me up—and that slogan! Our *true* queen? It makes me sound insufferable."

Frankie chuckled. "*Insufferable.* I like that word. Oh, come on, Emma, you know it's true. Autumn's the one who's too much to suffer."

Under different circumstances, I might have smiled at that. Autumn was a lot to *suffer.* But I wasn't through with Frankie yet.

"How did you even make this flyer into a poster?" I demanded.

"There's a poster machine at the high school. Mateo had Annie do it."

Annie was in on this? But then again, she probably didn't know that Frankie signed me up behind my back.

"You don't like Autumn any more than I do," Frankie was saying. Then he took my backpack from my shoulder and started walking toward the door. He really was the most confusing, and also kind of insufferable, person.

But did *I* want to run for queen? Frankie hadn't asked me before signing me up . . . but I *did* love the Valentine's dance.

I stopped walking, and Frankie did too. "Look," I told him, "I'm not sure if I'm going to run for queen or not. I'm going to have to think about it. But I don't like how you went behind my back and signed me up."

"Okay. Do what you want, I guess."

"I will!" I said. "And I can carry my own backpack."

With another shrug, Frankie handed me my bag.

I pushed past him and, walking fast, made my way out of school. Sometimes we walked home together, but just then I didn't really feel like waiting for him.

On the way home, I had a sudden impulse to stop at Morning Mugs. Maybe one of their delicious milkshakes would make everything seem just a little bit better.

When I pulled open the door, I was surprised to see Hallie sitting there . . . with Travis, of all people. She looked at me with kind of a guilty expression on her face. I saw that there was one of those big portfolio notebooks sitting on the table between them, and there were colored pencils everywhere, including a light blue one stuck behind Hallie's ear, and a red one between Travis's teeth. That one clattered onto the table when he opened his mouth to say, "Hey, Emma."

"I was just getting a milkshake," I said, feeling like I'd caught the two of them, somehow, even though it seemed pretty clear that they were working on the art project Travis had mentioned last week.

"You should sit with us," Hallie said, and started picking up pencils as Travis reached for the portfolio.

"No—you guys are working. I have to get home anyway—to let out Cupid." I was lying—Dad didn't have any classes today, and he could walk Cupid. "I was going to get my drink to go anyway."

"Okay. If you're sure," Hallie said, seeming sheepish. "You know, we still need to hit Morning Mugs like we were talking about. As soon as this project . . ."

"Of course!" I said. I stepped up to the counter and asked Shana for the vanilla milkshake that I no longer even really wanted.

It was probably stupid to feel jealous that Hallie would come here with Travis before the two of us got to have our catch-up visit. After all, it was perfectly obvious that they were actually working on a school project, and Mugs was a great place to do that.

When my milkshake was ready, I waved goodbye to Hallie and Travis. As I walked home sipping my thick, sweet shake, I promised myself a nice, quiet evening in front of the TV. I was all caught up on homework—and I didn't take art, so no project to work on right now. I didn't feel like seeing or talking to anybody else after the day I'd had.

When I walked in the back door to the kitchen, Ms. Bates was standing there wearing an apron and holding a wooden spoon. "Hi, Emma!" she said brightly.

I dropped my backpack on the floor, with a thud that seemed symbolic of both my mood and the entire day.

"Hi, Ms. B—Abby," I said.

"I'm cooking dinner for you and your dad," she said, totally unnecessarily, since I had working eyeballs and basic reasoning skills.

Cupid ran to greet me, and the furry kisses he planted on my face were the only part of my day so far that wasn't the absolute worst.

14

Autumn vs. Winters

Helping Ms. Bates prep dinner, and then hanging out to chat with her and Dad that night, had kept me from thinking too much about the Queen of Hearts thing. So, I hadn't actually figured out whether or not I wanted to run.

I'd told Frankie the truth: It wasn't my kind of thing. I preferred planning things behind the scenes. And I was truly annoyed that Frankie had made the decision for me.

But when I walked into the lobby at school the next morning and saw Autumn's latest tactic, I decided on the spot that I *would* run.

She'd put posters up all over the lobby—very fancy ones that she must have gotten made by a professional. Her new slogan was *TRUE* QUEEN? IF YOU WANT A QUEEN THAT DOESN'T ACT LIKE A PRINCESS, THEN VOTE FOR AUTUMN.

A princess? As if!

I wanted to rip all the posters down, but I knew I was way too much of a "good kid" to risk getting in trouble for doing something like that. Although at that moment, I wished I weren't.

Instead, I fumed all through first period, making lists of ideas for counter-slogans in my notebook.

Finally, just before the bell rang, I thought of a way to maybe turn the word *princess* around a bit.

Frankie was in my second-period class, so I went right up to his desk before class started. "Do you think you could get your brother to make some more posters?" I asked. I threw my notebook down on his desk. It was open to the page on which I'd written my new slogan idea in big block letters. VOTE EMMA WINTERS: THE PLANNING PRINCESS.

He raised an eyebrow. "So, I take it you *are* running?"

"It's a moral imperative now," I said. He looked a little confused. "It means Autumn basically dared me," I explained.

"Remind me to get you to help me study for our next vocabulary unit test, genius. *And* to never get you mad," he added with a grin.

I kind of wanted to point out that he had already gotten me mad by starting this whole queen business, but since I needed him to make the posters, I just nodded and took my seat.

"I can't believe you're actually going through with this," Hallie said to me at lunch. "You were really mad when Frankie signed you up to run!" I'd filled in Hallie on everything via text last night.

"I know . . . but Autumn . . . I just can't let her get away with this. Acts like a princess? *She's* the biggest princess of all time."

Hallie put down her sandwich. "I know she's a lot sometimes, but she's also one of your friends. We both went to her birthday party the last two years."

"Well, that was before. This is war now."

"Geez. You're taking this whole thing super seriously."

"It's the Valentine's dance!" I said, my voice going a bit shrieky. "It's practically the most important event of the year."

Hallie shrugged. "I'm not sure I'm even going to go."

"Wait, what? You have to!" I put down my milk, and a little sloshed out.

"I'm just not sure I'm into it this year."

"But you said you were looking forward to dancing this year at the dance."

"When did I say that?" Hallie asked.

My jaw dropped. How could she not remember?

"It was New Year's Day! The day Cupid fixed up Annie and Mateo."

"Em, that was weeks ago."

"Yes, but I was counting on you going."

"You don't need to go with me like the old days. I sort of assumed you'd take a date this year. Hasn't Frankie asked you?"

I frowned. "Um, sort of?"

Hallie narrowed her eyes. "What do you mean, sort of?"

"He mentioned it and implied that we could go together . . ."

"What did you say?"

As soon as Hallie asked the question, I realized that I'd been kind of considering it. Especially with all this queen race stuff, I really didn't want to go to the dance alone, or even just with a friend, like Hallie and I had done last year. It seemed that Frankie still would be open to going with me . . . maybe.

"I guess I haven't really answered him," I said at last.

"Well, maybe you should just *ask* him," Hallie said.

"Do you think so?"

"Emma, if you want to go with him, then, yes, you should. There's no law that says you can't."

I knew she was right, but something was still holding me back. When Frankie came to join us at our lunch table, as he did most days, I didn't bring up the dance. And neither did he.

"Cupid, I need your help. Just one more time—you need to do your magic!"

I held my pug up in front of my face and looked deeply into

his eyes as I explained my dilemma to him. "I need you to convince Hallie to go to the Valentine's dance. I cannot go alone. Which means you need to find a boy to ask her!"

Cupid blinked at me. I could only hope he understood. We sat on the carpet in my bedroom and I'd pulled out the HMS yearbook from last year. I plonked Cupid in front of its pages and waited to see if he would put a paw or a nose on one of the pictures. But as he snuffled around, coming back to me as though confused about what I wanted, he only put a paw on one photo: Vice Principal Jericho.

I would have to do the picking part myself, and then, if I chose well, maybe Cupid would work his magic. Which meant I'd need to get both Hallie and the boy I chose to come to my house.

I flipped through the pages for both seventh and eighth grade—people in my class or Theo's—over and over. The only boy who seemed like a decent possibility was Chris Thompson. After all, with the dance coming up so soon, a lot of boys had already asked someone. But Chris would do.

First, I texted Hallie to see if she was free the next day. Next, I went into the kitchen and found our school directory, then took a deep breath before calling Chris.

"Hi, Chris? This is Emma from school. Listen, I'm having a really small party tomorrow after school. I was hoping you could come."

"Ummmm," he mumbled. "At your house?"

"Yeah."

"Is it your birthday?"

"Kind of . . . it's not really a birthday party, but I just wanted to have some people over."

"Sure, I guess I can make it."

"You can? Great! See you then."

I hung up. Now I just needed to invite enough other people to make it plausibly seem like a small party and not just a fix-up for Hallie and Chris.

I texted Theo, and then my friends from class Izzie and Christina. Unfortunately, Izzie responded right away that she and Christina were both going shopping with Izzie's older sister, who was home visiting from college.

Just me and Hallie and Theo and Chris would be much too weird. I could invite Frankie, I supposed. I sent him a text.

One other idea came to mind, but it wasn't a great one. *But* maybe it was smart to keep your enemies close and all that. After all, even more than not losing to Autumn, the main thing I wanted from this whole queen contest disaster was for people not to see me as a snooty princess. Inviting my competition to my house seemed like a very non-princess thing to do. Right?

When both Autumn and Frankie texted back that they'd be there, I sat down to start planning. Cupid had fallen asleep with his head on my leg, so he was of course too cute to move. I reached out and grabbed a notebook from my desk and began to make a list of snacks to buy.

After we'd had snacks, I would get everyone playing games. And then, busy being the hostess, I would ask Hallie to walk Cupid for me, and of course she would need someone to keep her company . . . and there would be Chris! I smiled as I imagined the perfect match being made right there at my little party.

*   *   *

The next morning, I searched through my board games. I was determined to find one that would distract everyone, but also allow two players to leave in the middle. Nothing was quite right. I sat back on my heels as Cupid came snuffling over. Suddenly, I remembered a fun night with Theo's family last summer. We'd done the perfect thing: karaoke!

I just needed Theo to bring over his machine. I texted him and got back a thumbs-up sign. I texted him again:

But you have to come over early and set it up. The party starts RIGHT after school

Finally, after a ridiculously long wait, long enough for me to get dressed and begin eating my cereal, Theo texted back.

As you wish.

I'd take that as a yes.

Satisfied, I resumed eating my cereal with a smile. Cupid sat at my feet, waiting for his bite, and I realized I'd forgotten to save him a bite of dry cereal. I reopened the box.

"That dog is terribly spoiled," Dad said as he walked into the kitchen.

"No, he's *lucky*," I said.

"He certainly is. He has quite the doggy life." Dad poured himself some coffee. "You remember I have a department meeting tonight? I'll be late."

I stood up in alarm, nearly spilling my cereal. Cupid gave a short bark of worry. "But you said I could have friends over this afternoon!" I cried.

Dad frowned. "I did?"

"You did," I said.

"Shoot, Emma. Maybe another day . . . ?"

"There is no other day—everything is set. Dad, it *has* to be today."

He ran his hand through his hair. "I'm sorry, Emma, the meeting must have slipped my mind when you asked. But I'd like you to have an adult here if you have a big group of friends over . . ."

"What if we got Annie? I could pay her from my allowance . . ."

Dad had his thinking face on, considering my idea. "I suppose if Annie is willing to babysit, that would be all right."

"*Babysit!* Do we have to call it that?"

"It's just a figure of speech," Dad said. "The crucial thing here is that Annie is old enough to drive and has a car."

"Well, if that were the whole thing I could always call an Uber . . ." I saw Dad getting ready to object, so I jumped in and said, "*But* as long as you're saying yes, I'll go call Annie!" I raced upstairs.

"Emma Elizabeth Winters!" Dad called. "Your cereal bowl is just sitting here!"

"I'll be right back down!" I shouted.

Annie was a little confused that I was calling her to be my party babysitter, but she said she'd be happy to help. She said she still owed me for helping her meet Mateo.

"You don't owe me," I told her, although I privately thought that it really was down to me and Cupid that they'd met in such a romantic way.

When I found Theo before school, I reminded him to bring his karaoke machine to my house, and then at lunchtime I went over to his table to remind him again.

"Geez, Emma, I said I'll bring it."

I froze in surprise. Theo was never snappy like that. At least not to me.

"I'm sorry," he said right away, seeing my face. "I just . . . I wish you'd trust that I'll bring it after the first time you asked."

Autumn walked by our table and gave me a bright smile that didn't quite reach her eyes.

"Oh, hello, Emma. I'm really looking forward to your party. Thank you for inviting me. Maybe you should invite Tara Duncan, and then it can be a gathering of all the people running for queen. I didn't know you were interested in that," she added, her voice sounding less bright.

"I didn't either."

"Frankie signed her up for it," Theo said. He turned to me. "In fact, I kind of expected you to drop out."

"Well, he went to all that trouble with the posters and everything," I said, and the explanation sounded lame even to my own ears. "And the Valentine's dance is my very favorite event of the year," I added, which was true.

Theo gave me a strange look and then abruptly stood up and started taking his tray over to the trash cans.

Feeling confused, I turned back to Autumn. "Anyway, I'm so glad you can come today. Should be fun. Hopefully it won't rain." I waved goodbye to her as she walked away, and then I looked down and realized that I hadn't even started my lunch, Theo had left, and Hallie was nowhere to be found. Neither was Frankie.

"Hey, Emma," Travis said as he and Hallie came up to join me. Hallie set down that same giant art notebook I'd seen them working on at Morning Mugs.

"Hey," Hallie said. "We were working on our project. It's due soon."

"Cool," I said, just glad not to be sitting there alone, especially now that my face was on a flyer or a poster all over the school, calling myself the Planning Princess. Suddenly, that slogan, which had seemed so smart at the time, felt pretty embarrassing. Luckily, neither Hallie nor Theo had said anything about it to me.

All of a sudden, I was stuck with a terrible thought. Was Hallie going to invite Travis to the party? Had she already invited him? That would ruin everything.

"You've got my vote," Travis said, and it took me a few seconds to figure out what he was talking about.

"For queen—oh, thanks, Travis."

"Sure." He turned back to Hallie and showed her something in the large notebook. "So, the latest thing is I'm thinking of adding straps here," Travis told her, and Hallie leaned forward to see where he pointed.

"Oh, that's even more awesome. You're so talented, Travis!" she exclaimed.

I looked down at the notebook. I was surprised to see a very good drawing of a bright pink gown with an interesting, asymmetrical hemline.

"That's really good," I told him.

"Thanks," Travis said, looking pleased and maybe a little bit embarrassed. He folded up the notebook and launched himself off the bench. "Gotta go, I'll see you both later."

"Bye, Travis," Hallie called.

I watched Travis walk away, surprised by his hidden talent of designing dresses. "So, are you excited for later today?" I turned back to ask Hallie.

Now it was her turn to look confused. "Oh, the thing at your house. Sure."

I eyed Hallie's outfit as I unwrapped my chicken-and-avocado sandwich. She was wearing a pink T-shirt and jeans: a little plain for a party, if you asked me. But she did look nice in pink with her pale skin. And I didn't want to make her nervous by commenting on her clothes. "Shana and Stella are sending over some snacks from Morning Mugs," I told her.

"Yum," Hallie said as she unwrapped her sandwich.

I smiled, imagining Chris and Hallie walking hand and hand down the lane beside my house, my magical Cupid walking between them.

After my last class, I raced home, excited. Not even the damp and cloudy weather could ruin my mood. I'd gotten *so* many snacks, and that was even without whatever Shana and Stella were sending over.

Tearing open the back door, I greeted Cupid in the usual way, by crouching down to kiss and hug him.

Annie came up to the back door just moments after me. "Hi there," she said, walking in and smiling down at me and Cupid. "It's been so long since I sat for you! I forgot the drama of your daily reunion with Cupid, after being so cruelly separated for seven whole hours."

"It felt like longer," I told her as Cupid kissed my ear. "Thank you again so much for coming over, Annie. You're the best."

"No problem," Annie said. "Shana and Stella sent over a bunch of stuff—you can help me bring it in from the car. And best of all—cupcakes!"

"Thank goodness!" I said, laughing. Annie is well-known as a cupcake mega-fan.

In the driveway, we met Theo, who walked up holding a box that I assumed contained his karaoke machine. "Delivery for Emma Winters," he intoned. "Where do you want this thing?"

"What do you think? In the dining room? Or maybe the den."

"Your call. You are mistress of the house." Theo grinned at

Annie. "We're reading Charles Dickens in English class," he explained. Annie had babysat both of us plenty of times, so she and Theo also knew each other well.

"Ooh, I love Dickens. *A Tale of Two Cities*?" Annie asked as she balanced a couple of boxes in her arms and headed into the house.

"No, *Great Expectations*. That poor Pip."

"No spoilers!" I told him. "I'll be reading it next year." I turned to Annie. "He's impossible; he completely blew the endings of *To Kill a Mockingbird* and *Ender's Game* for me last year."

"Don't complain to me, I usually skip to the end first. I don't like surprises," Annie said.

"That's fully insane," Theo said.

"But you're the one who spoilers me," I told him.

"*Spoilers* is not a verb," Theo said, setting up the machine in the den. I helped him plug it in. "Hey, could you bring me a cupcake?"

"So much for me being mistress of the house," I grumbled.

"That's what the mistress of the house *does*. She's the hostess."

I laughed, realizing he was, as usual, right.

Annie and I had just finished arranging the mountain of snacks when Hallie arrived. As soon as she stepped in, Autumn appeared right behind her.

"Welcome, everybody!" I called. "Come on into the kitchen, we have so much food."

"Who else is coming?" Hallie asked me.

"Just two more," I said, and the doorbell rang. "Come on, Hallie and Cupid, let's get the door." I was hoping it was Chris and not Frankie. That way, he would be the obvious choice to accompany Hallie on her walk with Cupid.

I opened the door, and it was indeed Chris. Whew! He looked pretty cute in his blue polo shirt. And Cupid even ran to the door to see who it was and started wagging his tail. Everything was off to a good start.

"Thanks for inviting me, Em—aaaa-CHOO!" Chris doubled over in a giant sneeze. And then he tried to say my name again and sneezed three more times.

"Bless you!" I said. "Do you have a cold?"

Chris shook his head. "I—I didn't know you had a dog," he said, sneezing again loudly. "I'm—I'm allergic."

I looked at Hallie, and she seemed to be trying not to laugh. Poor Chris's nose was already turning red. This was *not* the way things were supposed to go.

Frankie walked in through the front door behind Chris, said, "Gesundheit," as Chris sneezed again, then walked around him and into the foyer.

"Where're the snacks, Emma?" he asked. "I totally skipped lunch."

I didn't know what else to do, so I closed the door and led Chris and Frankie to the kitchen.

"Can I get you some Benadryl?" I asked Chris, whose nose was now streaming. After all, as Theo had reminded me, I was the hostess.

We stuffed ourselves for about fifteen minutes, and then Theo suggested we start a round of karaoke.

Everyone trooped into the den, but Autumn touched my arm before we followed them. "So, Emma, I've been to your house a couple of times, but I've never gotten the full tour."

I resisted a frown. What kind of trick was this? "Okay," I

said, "I can show you the upstairs if you want." I led her toward the staircase and tried to think of what my dad told adults when they toured around the house.

But before I could start, Autumn said, "I really just wanted us to have a chance to talk. I wanted to warn you about the Queen of Hearts race."

I turned to face her halfway up the stairs. "What do you mean?"

Autumn sighed. "I *mean* that everyone knows I have this contest on lock. You should just drop out and save yourself the humiliation."

I felt my back stiffen. "What gives you that idea?"

"The *idea* is that nobody likes how you boss them around, Emma Winters. They're *not* going to vote for you."

My face felt very hot. I stood up as tall as I could, glad that I was one step higher than her on the stairs. "I don't know who you think goes around saying that—except for *you*," I replied. "But I'm sorry to tell you that I wouldn't drop out now if my life depended on it."

I began to march regally downstairs past her, but Autumn's

voice called after me, "Do you even have a date for the dance, Emma?" she asked.

My heart was beating fast, and I heard it echoing in my ears. I was sure my face was still red. Autumn had never been my favorite person, but it seemed like she was much more awful than I'd ever imagined. I ignored her and kept walking.

"What's wrong?" Theo asked, coming up beside me as I shuffled into the den.

I shook my head. I couldn't talk about it. Not with everyone—including Autumn—still here. She followed me into the den, smiling like we hadn't just had our unpleasant confrontation.

"Autumn, you need to sing next!" Chris was holding the karaoke mic out for her. He sneezed twice before saying to the rest of us, "She's really good. We're in—*achoo*—chorus together."

Autumn smiled widely. "Well, I wouldn't say so myself, but some people do say my voice reminds them of Ariana Grande."

I snorted loudly, and Theo shot me a look. The music started—it was indeed an Ariana Grande song, and Autumn began to sing. Her voice really wasn't bad, but she'd definitely oversold herself.

Frankie came up beside me and rolled his eyes. "Em, I hate to say it, but your party is dullsville." He spoke loudly over Autumn's singing. "I'm going to take off."

"Oh," I said in a small voice. Trying to save face, I added, "I can't blame you. Ariana *extra small* up there is a lot to take."

I hadn't expected her to hear me—I wasn't speaking as loudly as Frankie was. But Autumn had stopped singing. She flung the microphone down and started looking around for her coat.

"I'm off," Autumn announced angrily.

Theo glared at me. "If anyone wants a ride, my mom can take you," he said.

My stomach dropped. *Theo was ending my party? What was even happening?*

I bent to pick up Cupid for the comfort of a furry hug. Beside me, Chris sneezed again, loudly, and I jumped.

"I'm all set," Autumn announced, checking her phone. "My Uber is almost here—I'll wait outside."

I watched her walk out the door, with Frankie behind her.

"I think I'll take you u—*A-CHOO*—up on that ride," Chris said to Theo, wiping his nose.

"Me too," Hallie said. "Unless you need me to stay and help clean a bit?" she asked me.

I shook my head, feeling miserable. "I'll get the machine later," Theo told me, and didn't look back at me as he led the rest of my guests out the door.

Annie walked into the den a few minutes later. "Emma? All the noise stopped. Where'd everybody go?"

"Apparently, I shouldn't throw any more parties," I told her, fighting back tears. "I managed to chase all my guests away in just under three minutes."

"What happened?"

I shook my head as my throat tightened. Talking about it just then seemed impossible. "Can you just help me clean up? Please? I'm sorry to have to ask," I added.

Annie walked closer. "It's no problem, Emma. Now, why don't I start by wrapping up the rest of those cupcakes?" she said with a wink.

I gave a small laugh, but my heart wasn't in it. Not only had my matchmaking scheme failed utterly, now it seemed like Theo was mad at me. I wanted to call him and explain about the awful things Autumn had said to me, but maybe that would seem like I was just trying to make excuses. The fact was, I'd said something rude about Autumn. The hostess of a party should provide food and drink . . . *and* she shouldn't be rude to her guests.

I went to the kitchen and pulled out a trash bag. It was time to start cleaning up my mess.

15

Clueless

I felt wretched. Instead of sitting on my bed, I sat down on the floor in the corner of my room. Cupid followed me, curling up against my side with a contented sigh.

I sat there, staring out at the small sliver of window I could see from my corner, wallowing. I felt angry at Theo for abruptly ending my party over one tiny comment—but at the same time I felt worried and kind of sick at the thought that *he* might be mad at *me*. Or think less of me.

Autumn had been so horrible to me, but now I was the bad guy. It just wasn't fair.

And nothing had worked out the way I'd hoped. Chris and Hallie hadn't even noticed each other—although poor Chris didn't notice much at all with his sneezing. I said a silent prayer that I would never develop an allergy to dogs—and neither would Dad or Theo or Hallie. It seemed like the worst allergy in the world. Beside me, Cupid gave another little adorable puppy sigh as though he were agreeing with me.

"Emma!" I heard Dad's voice calling. Cupid's tail began to wag, but I didn't move. Soon Dad was peering into my room. "Uh-oh," he said when he saw me in the corner.

"Why uh-oh?" I asked, though my voice came out small and tired-sounding.

"Because you never sit down there unless you're feeling very blue. What's the problem? Why don't you come on out of there and tell me about it, and we can figure out a way to solve it."

"I'm not even sure what the problem is!" I moaned. "Or even if there's just *one* problem. Lately I just feel like I don't understand *anyone*. Not like I used to. Everything's just so complicated now."

I guess Dad gave up on getting me to come out of my corner

because he sat down on the floor across from me. He looked so silly with his legs folded like that, I might have laughed, but I was feeling too low. "Well, let's just start with one specific problem," Dad said.

"Okay," I said. "The Valentine's dance."

"What about it?" Dad asked patiently.

I shrugged. "Last year, the dance was so much fun. I went with Hallie, and everyone was there, and we all danced and ate cupcakes and it was so amazing. But this year . . . well, everyone started to pair up with official dates. I tried to find one for Hallie, because I knew she wanted to go to the dance, but I struck out both times. And I . . . well, I don't have one either," I added in an embarrassed rush.

"You don't need to have a date to have a good time," Dad pointed out.

"I know," I said. "But still . . . it would be nice if some boy would ask me."

Dad nodded. "Well, any boy who hasn't asked you is just missing out," he said.

"Thanks, but you're my dad—you have to say that."

Dad laughed. "It's true, though. Besides, Emma, if you want to go with someone to the dance—why not ask him yourself?"

"That's what Hallie said." I rubbed little circles into Cupid's tummy just the way he liked.

Dad nodded. "Hallie's a very bright girl, but I've always said that. You are too, Emma—it's just—these things are hard to figure out at the beginning. Well, actually, they're always hard, if I'm being honest."

I glanced up at him. "You and Ms. Bates?"

"Yes. Me and Ms. Bates. Sometimes . . . the timing's just not right."

I swallowed hard. Did that mean he and Ms. Bates had broken up? I wasn't sure if I felt relieved, or disappointed. I realized I felt more disappointed.

"Dad?"

"Yes, Emma?"

"I do really like Ms. Bates. I mean, Abby."

Dad smiled. "Me too, Emma. Now, why don't you climb out of there and we'll see if we can't solve at least one more of those problems. Over some ice cream, maybe?"

"Not frozen yogurt? You always say how it's a healthier option."

"I think this situation calls for real ice cream," he said.

Without even knowing it—or maybe he actually did know—Dad helped me with my *most* upsetting problem by inviting Theo to come get ice cream with us.

Theo walked into the kitchen as I was hooking on Cupid's halter so he could come with us. Dad was finishing up some emails in his study, so it was just me and Theo (and Cupid) for now.

"Hey," I said, feeling strange. The anger I'd been holding inside seemed mostly gone now.

"Hey," Theo replied, his hands in his pockets. He knelt down and rubbed Cupid's back as Cupid kissed his face.

"Listen, Theo—I . . . I'm sorry about before. I shouldn't have said that. But if you'd heard what Autumn had just said to me . . ."

Theo glanced up at me. "I figured she must have provoked you somehow. But, Emma—is that really how you want to handle stuff like that? Insulting her back, in public?"

I hung my head. I felt deflated—I'd been trying to recall Autumn's exact, horrible words so I could recite them back to Theo, and then he'd understand and forgive me. But *his* words had taken all the air out of me. He was right, I knew. Just because Autumn had been awful didn't mean I had to be awful too.

Cupid trotted back to me and jumped on his hind legs to get my attention. I knelt down to pat him and he licked my cheek.

With my free hand, I swiped at the hot tears that were forming in my eyes. "You're right," I told Theo.

Theo took a step forward. "Oh, Emma—please don't cry. I didn't mean to be hard on you. And I'm sorry about what happened earlier too. I didn't have to be so dramatic and leave so fast. It just seems like you've been . . . different. Since you've been spending so much time with, well, you know . . . with Frankie."

I looked up at him in surprise. "I thought you liked Frankie?"

Theo frowned. "I'm not saying I don't . . ."

"You kids ready?" Dad called, and Theo didn't finish his sentence.

"Yeah," I said, getting to my feet.

I led the way to the Creamery with Cupid trotting at my side. When we arrived, we all ordered our usual favorites. Now that it felt like things were mostly patched up between Theo and me, I felt so much better.

"Thanks, Dad," I told him as we walked outside with our cones. Theo was up ahead walking Cupid. "This was a good idea." He'd known just how to make me feel better.

"You're welcome, sweetie," Dad said, and gave me a kiss on the forehead.

Up ahead of us, Cupid turned around and gave a short bark, as if to say, *What about me?*

"I think someone is jealous he didn't get ice cream," Dad said with a smile.

Now that Theo and I were back on good terms, I knew I should make sure everything was okay with Hallie too. That night, as I wrote in my journal at my desk, I realized that there had been a sort of tension between us for a while. Instead of trying to fix it,

I'd just been glad whenever I'd managed to change the subject, or a distraction—like Theo—showed up. It was time to focus on Hallie, and do something nice for her.

I hopped online and carefully picked out everything that I knew would make Hallie look awesome for the dance: the perfect dress, shoes, and even a necklace. I also found a great hairstyle idea on YouTube. I texted Hallie and asked her to come over after school on Tuesday, which would give everything I ordered with two-day shipping a chance to arrive. And then I'd give her a surprise dance makeover!

Why *couldn't* the two of us just put on great outfits and go together like we had last year? It would be so much fun.

Hallie texted back a thumbs-up, and I felt lighter than I had in weeks. I lay down on the floor beside a snoozing Cupid.

"I know I told you that you needed to find a great date for Hallie for the dance," I told him. "But now I'm thinking just wait a little on that, okay, buddy?"

Cupid looked up at me drowsily, but I could almost swear he nodded before going back to sleep.

* * *

I surprised Hallie by opening the door wearing everything I planned to wear to the Valentines dance. "Surprise!" I said.

"I thought you said we were hanging out," Hallie said, sounding confused as she walked inside.

"We are!"

"If this is the new Winters family dress code, I have to say I won't be watching any more movies here," Hallie said drily.

"No, silly, this is your surprise. Come on!" I pulled her along upstairs with me.

In my bedroom, Cupid looked up from his fluffy purple bed and then came running to greet Hallie.

She knelt down to pet him, still looking up at me with a wary expression. "What's this about, Em?"

"It's a Valentine's makeover!" I announced. "I have a surprise for you. I've been thinking, we don't need dates to the dance. We can just get all dressed up and go together—just like last year. We had so much fun."

I closed my bedroom door to reveal the purple dress I'd picked for her hanging on the back of it. "Surprise!"

Hallie crossed her arms. "What is that?"

"It's a dress, silly!"

"I mean . . . who is it for?"

"For you, of course." I looked down at my own red dress. "I'm wearing this one. I already showed you—remember?"

Hallie nodded. "Yeah. I remember. I made you earrings to match it, remember? But you're not wearing them."

I felt my face turn pink. I realized then that I'd completely forgotten about the earrings she'd given me a few weeks ago. "Oh," I said. "I mean, they were really pretty, but for the dance and with this dress, I decided not to wear something homemade."

Hallie's face turned pink too. "Ah. Got it. Well, then I guess you're not going to want to be seen with me at the dance, because my whole dress is going to be *homemade*. That's the project Travis and I have been working on."

She opened the door and took a step out. I followed her, my heart pounding in my chest. "Wait—Hallie—I'm sorry—I didn't mean . . ."

She whirled back to face me, more color in her cheeks than before. "I know what you meant. But I'm excited about the dress

Travis and I designed. His mom is sewing it for me. Oh, and by the way, I've been trying to figure out a way to tell you this for a while: I *have* a date to the dance. Travis and I are going together."

Her words made the floor shift under my feet. She'd been trying to tell me for a while? All this time I'd been trying to find Hallie the perfect date; how long had she already had one?

"I—I don't understand," I sputtered. "Why didn't you tell me?"

Hallie set her jaw. "Because of how you're looking at me right now," she said. "You can't stand Travis because of what he did at the festival last year. And I know it was dumb—*he* knows it was dumb. But he was trying to help with that horse and the hayride. His dog is a rescue, and he was trying to get him used to crowds. But the horse ended up scared and his dog did too. It's not like he was trying to ruin everything."

I looked over at Cupid and realized how lucky I was that my dad had been able to get us a dog trainer when Cupid was tiny. Travis wasn't a bad owner. He'd rescued his dog, after all.

"I'm going to go," Hallie said. "You can return that dress. I'm going to wear the one we designed. And you don't have to wear the earrings. You can just throw them away."

With that, she was gone. I stood frozen. I wanted to chase after her, to apologize, to somehow make it right, but by the time I could make my feet move, it was too late.

I sank down onto the floor, wrinkling my fancy dress and then not even caring when Cupid scrambled into my lap and got dog hair all over it.

I realized, in that moment, that I'd been completely, totally, epically clueless about everything. I'd also been a really terrible friend. I kept hearing Hallie's final words echo in my head. *You can just throw them away.*

Finally, I got to my feet, wriggled out of my dress and changed, then kissed Cupid goodbye. I shrugged into my coat and started walking.

I'd been so misguided—and about more than just Hallie. I could see it all now. It was like Hallie's words had taken a pair of rose-colored glasses off my eyes and I could see everything clearly.

And then it hit me: All that scheming I'd done to try to get Cupid to find Hallie a date for the dance had been pointless . . . because Cupid had already picked Travis for Hallie.

I remembered it so clearly now. All the way back at the winter carnival, Cupid had done his "trick" and given each of them a wet, sloppy kiss! But I'd been so blinded by my dislike of Travis that I hadn't even noticed.

Speaking of being blinded, part of me couldn't believe I'd been considering Frankie's half offer to go to the dance with him. Cupid certainly hadn't ever done his little trick on *us*. I thought of Frankie carrying my books, winking at me, and even signing me up for the queen race. Of course, I really hadn't wanted Frankie to do that. I was embarrassed now thinking of those awful signs I'd asked Frankie to make, which were hanging all over the school.

I found myself walking up to Theo's house, but I couldn't bear to knock on the door.

Out of everything I felt bad about, the worst part was thinking about what Theo would say, and how his face would look, when I had to tell him how awful and insensitive I'd been to Hallie.

Theo really was the best. And not just because he was always trying to get everyone to be more responsible about the environment, or more socially aware. He was always nice to everyone—even Frankie, even though it seemed like maybe he didn't actually like Frankie that much. And for me, Theo was the one who always made me realize when I was being too controlling, or even not being nice. All he had to do was look at me, and I knew what he was thinking.

I looked up at Theo's window, just for a few seconds. Then I turned away and kept walking. I couldn't admit to Theo how badly I'd acted—especially now.

Before I could really face him again, I had to give myself a makeover. Not a dance makeover—a be-a-better-person makeover.

I didn't have it all figured out, but I started walking faster toward home because I realized I did know one place I could start.

16
Cooking Looks Easy on TV

I dumped the pasta out of the pot and into the strainer, feeling the steam hot on my face. Were the noodles supposed to clump together like that?

I was cooking what had seemed like a simple, easy recipe for Dad and Ms. Bates—hopefully. Dad was coming back from a meeting on campus, and I was going to ask him if Ms. Bates could come over too.

Because I decided on my realization walk yesterday that one other thing I'd been blind to was my dad.

When he was comforting me the other day, Dad had said

something, and I'd been too wrapped up in my own misery to really listen. He'd told me that relationships weren't easy at any age, and he'd said, *Sometimes the timing's just not right.*

It made sense now. Ms. Bates had stopped coming around. And at school, she'd seemed to lose that spark of happiness she had when she and Dad first started seeing each other. The past week or so she'd seemed rather blue.

I wondered if when Dad talked about timing with him and Ms. Bates what he really meant was *me*. Surely he had noticed when I kept making excuses not to go out to dinner with them. He'd noticed that I kept calling her Ms. Bates instead of Abby (although that part wasn't easy—I still *thought* of her as Ms. Bates, even in my head).

I was worried Dad had decided that *I* wasn't ready, and he'd backed off from seeing Ms. Bates. But I wanted to ask him first—to see what he wanted before I made plans for the two of them. After all, maybe I was totally wrong about the whole thing, and this idea was destined to go as badly as my chicken piccata was going.

I wiped my flour-dusted arm across my forehead and frowned

down at the mess I was making. Cooking looks so easy on TV.

The back door opened, and Dad walked in.

"Emma—what's all this?"

"Surprise!" I said weakly. "I was trying to cook dinner for you. For you and Ms. B—I mean, Abby. If you wanted to invite her. But I think . . . I think it may be a disaster."

"Oh, what a lovely surprise, Emma," Dad said with a crooked smile. He came over to look at my attempts. "That's so nice of you. What are you cooking?"

"Chicken piccata."

"Are those olives?" Dad asked, surveying the ingredients that were strewn across the counter.

"Yes. You can use those in place of capers, right?"

"Well, I don't really know, but you know who would?"

"Abby?" I asked hopefully.

Dad nodded. "You were doing this for us?" he asked me.

"Yeah," I said. "I noticed she hasn't been coming over anymore. And I know maybe there's other stuff going on, but if it's because of me . . . I don't want that. I really like her, Dad. And I want you to be happy. Even if it's a little weird."

Dad's face lit up. "Thanks for saying that, Emma. I'll give her a call. But maybe we could take a rain check on the cooking?" He glanced down at my "meal" again. "For tonight, how about one of those pizzas you're so good at ordering? And we could rent a movie."

I nodded, taking off my apron while Dad called Ms. Bates. By the time he got off the phone, he was grinning.

"She'd love to come have pizza with us. She said she loves veggie. And that she'd be happy to give you a cooking lesson sometime!"

I laughed and said, "I'd love that, Dad. I'll order a large veggie pizza?"

Cupid gave a short bark of protest. "I'll order a small sausage too," I whispered to him with a wink.

When Abby arrived, after Cupid finished giving her a furry welcome, she announced that she had a surprise for both Dad and me. She pulled her laptop out of her bag and hit a few keys before standing back and saying, "Ta-da!"

Dad and I stepped forward to see. Abby had pulled up an

image: a drawing of the outside of a building. The sign said ABBY'S BOOKS.

I looked at Dad's face to see if he knew anything about this. But he was looking at Abby and asking, "What's this?" in a surprised voice.

Abby smiled. "This is something I've been working on for a while now. Both of you actually helped me realize that opening my own bookstore was the right next step for me. Emma, when I got to go with you on your trip to New York, I realized that what I *really* wanted was to be around writers and writing."

I nodded. That made sense.

"It's not so much about living in New York—it's about surrounding myself with what inspires me," Ms. Bates went on. "As much as I love working at the school and being a librarian, I'm ready for a new challenge. And, James"—she turned to face Dad—"you made me realize how much I have here in Highbury, and how much I really do want to stay."

I wasn't even bothered by seeing Abby and my dad smile at each other mushily. I was just happy Ms. B—Abby was happy.

"That's amazing," my dad told her.

Ms. Bates glanced at me. "What do you think, Emma?"

"I'll miss you so much at school," I said truthfully. "But I know I'll be seeing a lot of you!" She and Dad grinned at each other even more broadly. "Do you think maybe I could help you plan your bookstore? After all, you know how much I love to plan . . ."

Abby reached over and gave me a hug. "I do. And I was counting on it."

Cupid gave a happy bark. "You're going to be a bookstore mascot, Cupid!" I told him. Dad shook his head, but he was still smiling, and Abby and I both knelt down to give Cupid a double pet in celebration.

17

More Makeover

The next phase in my plan started bright and early the next morning. It felt good taking down all those "Planning Princess" posters, and replacing them with the simple ones I'd made at home, using a pretty drawing of a leaf Hallie had left on my desk and the slogan TURN OVER A NEW LEAF AND VOTE FOR AUTUMN.

Frankie came up beside me as I was shoving a pile of posters into the trash.

"Oh, hey," I said, feeling awkward.

"So, I guess you're not running after all," he said.

"No. I never really wanted to. I just got really . . . competitive there for a second, after Autumn told me I wouldn't win. I am sorry that you made the posters for nothing."

Frankie shrugged. I realized he did that a lot. "Whatever. I guess you don't really have the killer instinct. I don't think you're really who I thought you were at all, actually. Later."

I stood staring after him. His words really didn't sting like they probably would have even a few days ago. I just felt sort of . . . relieved. Around Frankie, I was not the best Emma I could be. It wasn't his fault. But it also didn't really make me want to be around him that much.

I still liked him in a lot of ways. He could be really funny. And he was a great soccer player. I thought back to when I'd first met Frankie, and Mateo. Maybe his big brother being mean to him had made him turn a bit snarky. Or maybe he just had a lot of growing up to do. That part, I could definitely understand.

In first period, Autumn came up to my desk and stood in front of it with her arms crossed. "What are you up to, Winters?"

I looked up at her. "I dropped out of the race."

"Okay . . . but why would you do that?" she demanded.

"From what I heard, you were ahead. Which I found shocking, but anyway . . ."

"I'm sorry," I said. "For being so rude to you at my party. I was angry at the things you said to me, but that's still no excuse. I never really wanted to be queen—I just got caught up in it for a while. But I know it's important to you. The signs were my way of saying sorry—and helping. No offense to Tara Duncan, but you're my friend. I'd rather see you win."

Autumn opened her mouth but no words came out. Finally, when she spoke, she said, "I . . . really? You still think of us as friends?"

"If you'll forgive me, then yes, I do."

"I'm sorry too," Autumn said. "I was such a jerk to you about the queen race. I really did—I do want to win. But I was still wrong to act the way I did. Can you forgive me?"

I nodded and smiled. "Forgiven. As long as you promise never to remind me of the whole 'Planning Princess' thing . . . like, ever."

"Deal," Autumn said, shaking my hand, then pulling me to my feet for a hug.

Well, that was one friendship mended.

Now I still had the most important one to go. And it wouldn't be as easy as tearing down some signs and dropping out of the race.

Hallie didn't sit with me at lunch again that day. But I couldn't really say I was surprised, or that I blamed her. I thought about trying to apologize, or putting a note in her locker, but those both seemed lame after how I'd acted. I decided that I needed to *show* her I was trying to be a different, better person.

Of course, even though I hadn't told Theo about our fight, he clearly noticed Hallie not sitting with me or talking to me.

He left the table of his soccer friends and came to sit down beside me when he spotted me alone.

"What's going on with you and Hallie?" he asked right away. Theo always knew exactly what was going on with me, even when I didn't say a word.

"I messed up," I admitted.

"What did you do?"

"Well, I . . . Don't make me tell you about it yet—okay?" I

said, playing with my sandwich wrapper. "It's just—I know I was wrong and I can't bear to see that look on your face. Not yet. But I do need your help. I need to show Hallie that I can be a good friend to her. And to Travis. That I'm happy they're going to the dance together."

"They're going together?" Theo asked, seeming surprised but not as much as I had been.

"Yes. And Hallie explained that last fall, at the carnival . . . Travis was still training his dog, which is why it all turned into such a mess. It wasn't a prank; it was just an accident. I guess his dog is a rescue."

"Yeah." Theo nodded. "I knew that."

I blushed; I'd thought I knew everything there was to know about everyone in Highbury.

"I was thinking of making a donation—like to an animal shelter—in Travis's name?" I said haltingly.

"Aw, that is a great thought, Em," Theo said. "Or you could even think about volunteering at the shelter?"

"You're right!" I cried, and slapped a hand to my forehead. "Why didn't I think of that?"

Theo fake-dramatically cleared his throat. "Well, I am . . ."

"I know. A whole year older." I rolled my eyes, even though I secretly loved the joke. The familiarity of Theo would always be comforting.

"Do you want me to come with you?" Theo said.

"Honestly? Yes. But . . . I think maybe this is something I should do on my own."

"I think you're probably right," he said, taking a big bite of his sandwich. "But if you need help finding a place, you could ask my mom."

"*That* I think I will do," I said. "Thanks, Theo." As we sat just the two of us at the cafeteria table, I realized who it was that *did* help make me the best Emma I could be: Theo. While Frankie tried to make me someone I wasn't, Theo had always known just who I was. It was his patience that helped me figure out what I needed to do. I glanced over at his green eyes and suddenly felt my stomach swoop. Maybe there was one more thing that I hadn't seen right in front of me.

"Anytime." Theo smiled.

*   *   *

Theo's mom told me about a shelter downtown that I could walk to. I knew it was there, of course, but I'd never really paid much attention. She said they were always in need of help at this time of year, and suggested I ask for her friend Mindy.

When I got there, I gave Mindy the donation money I'd brought. It was all the money I got returning all the stuff I'd bought for the dance for Hallie, and everything I had saved from my allowance. "Can I make the donation in someone's name?" I asked her.

"Of course," Mindy said.

I gave her Travis's name, and then Mindy put me to work cleaning dog crates. She showed me how to hose them off, then use a brush to scrub between all the metal grates, then hose them again, and finally set them in the sun to dry. It was hard work, but it felt good to lose myself in it.

As I scrubbed, I thought about what I'd started to realize at lunch. Could I actually, maybe, *like* Theo? I'd never thought about him that way before, but we'd been friends for so long. All I knew was that my heart raced when I thought about things changing between us—maybe because that would be a scary change. But lately I'd been trying to accept that change could also be good.

After I finished at the dog shelter, I thanked Mindy and headed home. I was tired, but feeling better about myself, as I walked in the door.

I gave Cupid an extra-tight hug, thinking of all those cute little furry faces at the shelter, hoping for their forever homes. I began to wonder if I could do more to help them. If I, as a native Highburian, had never thought very often of the place, maybe they needed some publicity. Maybe an event, something like our school carnivals, but as a fund-raiser . . . I began to plan out ideas in my head.

A few days later, Travis came up to me at my locker. "I got this card," he said. "It says you made a donation in my name to the Prince Street Shelter?"

I nodded. "I hope you don't mind. I volunteered there the other day, and it was great. Hallie told me your dog is a rescue, which gave me the idea."

"Yeah, that's the shelter where we got Boxer!" Travis said, perking up at the mention of his dog. "He was pretty shy when we brought him home. That's part of how that whole disaster at the carnival happened." He made a sheepish face. "But now that he's used to us, he's doing so much better."

"I'm glad," I said. I wondered if Cupid and Boxer would get along.

"Hey, do you mind if I tag along and volunteer too?" Travis asked. "It would be nice to give back, since they rescued Boxer."

I blinked in surprise. "Sure. I mean, I'm going after school today. You could meet me."

"Cool. See you then."

I watched him walk away. It certainly seemed like a good sign. But it still didn't fix everything between me and Hallie, I knew.

I swallowed hard, thinking again about how it felt with her ignoring me, not eating lunch with me. We'd eaten lunch together practically every day since the fourth grade.

Suddenly, I couldn't bear the thought of having lunch in the cafeteria without her. At least not today. I went to the library and asked Abby if she minded if I read a book there while I ate my sandwich. You're not supposed to eat in the library, but she made a special exception for me. I guess there are some perks to having the librarian go out with your dad.

When I walked in the door to the Prince Street Shelter that afternoon, there was a surprise waiting for me. Hallie was standing there with Travis, and I could tell by her expression that she was going to forgive me. Maybe not all at once, right now, but by the time I reached her, there were tears in both our eyes and we were hugging each other tightly.

"I'm so sorry," I said.

"I'm sorry too, Em," Hallie said. "I know how much work you put into that fall carnival, and if I really wanted you to understand about Travis, I should have explained."

"I'm sorry three," Travis said, stepping forward. "For bringing Boxer to the carnival and managing to let that horse free . . . Boxer wasn't ready for that crowd yet."

I swiped away some tears. "It's okay. I'm glad Boxer didn't

get hurt. I guess it would have been kind of funny if I weren't so obsessed with planning everything perfectly and controlling every last thing." I turned to Hallie. "I'm going to work on not doing that as much."

Hallie smiled and wiped away some tears of her own. "That sounds good to me."

I pulled my phone out of my pocket and texted her our secret emoji.

She texted one back too, plus some hearts.

I hugged her again. Travis came in to the hug too and I had to laugh. I knew if Cupid were there, he would have jumped up on my legs, eager to join in the fun.

Hallie, Travis, and I worked hard cleaning cages and litter boxes for a few hours. We all admired the cuteness of the animals, and Travis and I talked about how we wished we could have more than one pet. I wondered if Cupid would be open to having a little furry sibling someday.

When Travis's mom came to pick him up, Boxer bounded out of their van, and I gave him some extra apology petting. How could I ever have been so snooty about a dog? As he ran between all three of us, I could tell that he, and my friends, had forgiven me.

I came home to a note from Dad saying he'd be back in a few minutes, that he'd taken Cupid with him to the pharmacy drive-through. It was nice of him to let Cupid ride along.

The house was quiet. I walked upstairs, feeling lighter than I'd felt in days, now that things were patched up with Hallie.

I saw something on the floor at the edge of my closet and went to pick it up. It was the scarf that had been my mom's, the one I'd worn to Frankie's birthday dinner.

How had it fallen down? I picked it up, feeling the soft, silky fabric. At that moment, it seemed almost like a small message from my mom, telling me that she was still watching over me.

I pulled out my journal, suddenly inspired to write about how much I missed her, how much I hoped she was still with me.

I wrote and wrote, the words coming easily now. It felt good to get some of the feelings down on paper. I didn't think I'd ever show this entry to anyone, but it still felt good to write it all down.

Closing the journal, I wrapped the scarf around my neck, not caring that it didn't match what I was wearing. I'd always wondered if my mother would have been proud of me. Right at that moment, somehow, I felt sure that she was.

18

Cupid's New Clothes

"Are you sure you don't want to come with me and Travis? You love the Valentine's dance! And I'm planning to tear up that dance floor!" Hallie sounded excited over the phone as I sat on the couch with Cupid. He snuffled against my side, and I gave him a pat.

"Get Travis to take some video of that and text it to me," I said. "But I think I'm going to spend a quiet evening here with my favorite date—Cupid."

I'd heard a few days ago that Theo had asked Katelyn Gold to the dance, and even though I was trying very hard to be a better person, I could admit to myself that I didn't really want to see him dancing with another girl. Every time I'd seen him the last couple of days, I'd tried to act like nothing had changed while my heart started to race. It felt weird to feel so, well, *weird* around Theo.

"Okay, if you're sure," Hallie said. "I have to go finish getting ready."

"Send a pic of your dress!" I said. "I'm sure it's gorgeous. You and Travis are both really talented," I added, meaning it.

"Thanks, Em. Talk to you soon."

"Have fun!" I hung up, and suddenly the silence in the house seemed a little overwhelming. Dad was out on a date with Abby. Beside me, Cupid yawned and fell back to sleep.

And I was suddenly second-guessing my decision to stay home. I thought about how beautiful all my friends would look in their dresses.

Then there was a knock on the back door.

Cupid perked up and beat me to the door. On the other side stood Theo, who would normally never knock. I saw he was wearing a suit, and I was even more confused.

He knelt down to greet Cupid first and, as usual, received a big wet puppy kiss. And then my magic little pup came back to me and I scooped him up in my arms, where Cupid gave me kisses as well.

Wait.

Realization struck me then.

All this time, had Cupid been doing his special "matchmaking" trick . . . on *me and Theo*?

I thought back to all the times when Theo had come over and Cupid had given kisses to him and then me, or vice versa. Had my smart pug been sending signs all along that I'd never noticed? Did Cupid agree with what I'd just recently been thinking—that Theo was a perfect match for me?

My heart was racing, but I tried to act like nothing was out of the ordinary.

"Hi," I said to Theo, setting Cupid down.

"Hey, can I come in?" Theo asked.

"Sure. Won't you be late for the dance, though?" I asked, feeling a little awkward as I stepped back to let him in. I wondered why he was stopping here before picking up Katelyn.

"Probably a little, but don't they say it's fashionable to be late?"

"I guess so," I said. He looked so handsome in his suit. He was carrying a bag. Had he brought me food or something? This was all so strange.

"So, I brought you something." Theo met my eyes for the first time, and I realized he seemed sort of . . . nervous.

"Oh. Okay. Thank you," I said, accepting the bag Theo held out to me. Cupid cocked his head and watched me with curiosity.

I opened up the bag. Inside I found a tiny dog tuxedo and a tiny top hat. "You brought me clothes for Cupid?"

As much as I loved dressing up my dog, at that moment, the thought of staying home and putting him in a tiny suit and top hat while all my friends went to a real dance seemed terribly pathetic.

"It's so he can go with us. To the dance."

I looked up at Theo as I played the words back in my head. He'd said *so he can go with* us. "But I thought you were going with Katelyn?"

"Who told you that?"

Now that I thought about it, I thought it might have been Frankie. "I'm not sure."

"Well, I was never going with Katelyn. I wanted to go with you," Theo said, his cheeks turning red. He took a deep breath and added, "But I thought you liked Frankie Castillo."

"I thought I might've too, for a little while."

"So, you don't like him?"

"I feel bad saying this . . . but I sort of *don't* like him. Sometimes he's not very nice."

Theo grinned. "I couldn't agree more. But maybe he just has some growing up to do," Theo added, which was exactly what I'd been thinking the other day about Frankie. But then again, Theo always did try to see the best in everyone.

"Hey, so now that we've talked about Frankie way more than I planned to—what do you say? Come to the dance with me?" Theo's green eyes met mine hopefully.

I smiled. "I'd love to," I said, meaning it with all my heart. Cupid let out a happy bark, and I shook my head. "But, Theo—Cupid can't come to the dance. The school won't allow it."

"I got special permission. Remember, you've got a special connection."

I frowned. "But Abby's out with Dad."

"They're chaperoning the dance and then going out to dinner." Theo grinned.

"You arranged this?"

"Guilty."

I guess I wasn't the only one capable of making plans.

I dropped the bag of doggy clothes and threw my arms around Theo. He really was the absolute best.

His arms slowly closed around me. Finally he pulled back. "So, I take it that's a yes? About the dance?"

"It's a yes. Give me ten minutes!" I said, letting go and running upstairs.

I ran halfway back down a few seconds later to yell, "You dress Cupid. And make that twenty!"

I heard Theo's chuckle follow me back up the stairs.

In the end, I wore the dress I'd worn on New Year's, since, in my heart of hearts, I'd really wanted Theo to see me in it way back then. Luckily my New Year's dress also matched the earrings that Hallie had made for me, and there was no way I wasn't wearing those tonight.

Theo, Cupid, and I walked over to the school and entered the gym. It was decorated beautifully—with pink and red balloons and streamers. I was proud of the work I'd put in.

"You came after all!" Hallie shrieked when she saw me, Theo, and Cupid walk into the gym. She ran over and threw her arms around me. "With Theo, huh?" she whispered in my ear mischievously. "About time."

"What do you mean?" I asked, blushing.

"I've been waiting for you to wake up," Hallie said.

I laughed. Apparently Hallie and Cupid knew me better than I knew myself. "I found out recently I can be pretty clueless sometimes, huh?"

"You are *usually* brilliant. But yes, once in a while, you can be a little clueless. We love you anyway, though," Hallie said, gently touching the earrings she'd given me. "These earrings are smashing, by the way," she added with a wink.

"Thank you," I said with a grin. "I think they look even better with this dress, actually."

"You know, I think so too."

We hugged again, and I gave Travis a high five and

complimented him on the design of Hallie's dress. He actually blushed a little as he said thank you, then showed me the latest picture of Boxer on his phone.

Autumn was already wearing her Queen of Hearts crown, and she waved happily at me from across the gym. Standing beside her was her date—Frankie. I had to laugh at that. Of course Autumn and Frankie had found each other—they were actually kind of perfect together.

I looked down at Cupid. "From now on, I'll leave the matchmaking to *you*," I whispered to him.

Cupid himself was the belle of the ball, sitting up in his stroller in his finery. Everyone came by to coo at him and pet him. While Cupid was being watched over by Abby and Dad—and avoided by poor Chris Thompson, whose sneezes I heard echoing across the gym—Theo led me out onto the dance floor.

"You know, I'm kind of glad you get to see my New Year's dress," I said to him shyly, reaching up to put my arms around his neck.

"I knew you were mad I missed New Year's," he said, pulling me just a little bit closer.

"Only because I missed you," I admitted. "I always miss you when you go away."

"But I always come back," Theo said.

"You'd better," I told him in a mock growl, and then he surprised me for the second time that night by leaning in closer to kiss me. The rest of the gym disappeared. All the kids, even the music, went silent as Theo and I kissed. My first kiss—and the most amazing one I could ever imagine.

Then the world restarted again and I was standing there with my very best friend—and the boy I adored.

"Speaking of travel, I have some news," I announced. I'd been sitting on the secret since yesterday. "I'm actually going somewhere this summer. So, you'll have to try not to miss *me* too much."

Theo's eyes widened. "Did you apply for the Society of Letters summer program after all?"

I nodded. "I did—and I just got the news that I was accepted!"

Theo picked me up and twirled me right around then. "Emma—I'm so proud of you!"

"I realized after hearing those other kids read their pieces that I have a lot of work to do if I really do want to be a better writer," I confessed. "Thank you for coming with me that day. I'm so glad I got to go. That trip—even though it was short, it was really important to me."

"I've always told you that travel is very important to personal growth," he said seriously.

I rolled my eyes. "Yes, I know, and you're so wise because you're . . ."

"A whole year older," we finished in unison.

I laid my head against Theo's shoulder with a happy sigh. I heard Cupid's short bark of approval from his spot at the edge of the dance floor. I glanced over to give my pug a smile.

He really is a very magical dog.

Acknowledgments

It is a truth universally acknowledged that a single author working in solitude cannot produce a truly excellent story. As always, thank you, Aimee Friedman and Olivia Valcarce, for the insight, ideas, good humor, and of course #pugpuns.

Thank you to my awesome agent, Devin Ross, and to everyone at New Leaf.

Yaffa Jaskoll, thank you so much for designing another pugdorable cover.

As Jane Austen wrote, "It's such a happiness when good people get together"—here's to my good friends Nikki, Beth, Carol, Mandy, Jeff, Sarah, and Gaby. <3 you guys.

Thank you PBDA family for your support, and for always being awesome.

And thanks, Mom, for our daily call. Talk to you tomorrow.

Have you read all the *wish* books?

☐ *Clementine for Christmas* by Daphne Benedis-Grab

☐ *Carols and Crushes* by Natalie Blitt

☐ *Snow One Like You* by Natalie Blitt

☐ *Allie, First at Last* by Angela Cervantes

☐ *Gaby, Lost and Found* by Angela Cervantes

☐ *Sit, Stay, Love* by J. J. Howard

☐ *Pugs and Kisses* by J. J. Howard

☐ *Pugs in a Blanket* by J. J. Howard

☐ *The Love Pug* by J. J. Howard

☐ *The Boy Project* by Kami Kinard

☐ *Best Friend Next Door* by Carolyn Mackler

☐ *11 Birthdays* by Wendy Mass

☐ *Finally* by Wendy Mass

☐ *13 Gifts* by Wendy Mass

☐ *The Last Present* by Wendy Mass

☐ *Graceful* by Wendy Mass

☐ *Twice Upon a Time: Beauty and the Beast, the Only One Who Didn't Run Away* by Wendy Mass

☐ *Twice Upon a Time: Rapunzel, the One with All the Hair* by Wendy Mass

- [ ] *Twice Upon a Time: Sleeping Beauty, the One Who Took the Really Long Nap* by Wendy Mass

- [ ] *Blizzard Besties* by Yamile Saied Méndez

- [ ] *Random Acts of Kittens* by Yamile Saied Méndez

- [ ] *Playing Cupid* by Jenny Meyerhoff

- [ ] *Cake Pop Crush* by Suzanne Nelson

- [ ] *Macarons at Midnight* by Suzanne Nelson

- [ ] *Hot Cocoa Hearts* by Suzanne Nelson

- [ ] *You're Bacon Me Crazy* by Suzanne Nelson

- [ ] *Donut Go Breaking My Heart* by Suzanne Nelson

- [ ] *Sundae My Prince Will Come* by Suzanne Nelson

- [ ] *I Only Have Pies for You* by Suzanne Nelson

- [ ] *Shake It Off* by Suzanne Nelson

- [ ] *Confectionately Yours: Save the Cupcake!* by Lisa Papademetriou

- [ ] *My Secret Guide to Paris* by Lisa Schroeder

- [ ] *Sealed with a Secret* by Lisa Schroeder

- [ ] *Switched at Birthday* by Natalie Standiford

- [ ] *The Only Girl in School* by Natalie Standiford

- [ ] *Once Upon a Cruise* by Anna Staniszewski

- [ ] *Deep Down Popular* by Phoebe Stone

- [ ] *Revenge of the Flower Girls* by Jennifer Ziegler

- [ ] *Revenge of the Angels* by Jennifer Ziegler

Fall for these adorable stories of sweet pugs and first crushes

scholastic.com/wish

WISHPUGS